Once Upon a Pacific Island

(The McKay Saga, Volume One)

by

Ken Ralls

Chapter One
The Island

This is a perfect moment for us to see the island for the first time.

Although it was not yet daylight on the *Sarah*, Dan saw the first rays of sunlight strike the top of the extinct volcano, then rapidly move down its eastern slope until the whole island would be revealed to those on the yacht as the sun emerged from the sea.

"Good morning, Sarah. Is this a perfect introduction, or what?" asked Dan as his wife appeared from below deck with a freshly brewed cup of coffee for her husband, her blue eyes still looking sleepy.

"Good morning. Beautiful! Just beautiful! Oh, I love it already, Dan!" she said, enjoying the island bathed in the brilliance of a Pacific sunrise. "Too bad the kids aren't up here to see. The volcano is awesome. This looks like places I used to imagine when we were listening to Martin Denny's band at *Don the Beachcomber's* on Waikiki Beach in Hawaii. Remember?"

"Oh, yeah! Exotic!"

When Dan had been stationed in Hawaii at Barber's Point Naval Air Station, they had stopped by many evenings at Don the Beachcomber's to listen to Martin Denny's group playing exotic tropical music.

"And imagine what it must have been like here when the volcano was active!" added Sarah.

The murmur of voices topside had roused the

rest of the McKay family and soon the twins, Luke and Laura, who had just turned sixteen, were hustling up to enjoy the scenery also. The twins were typical of youth their age...very vocal.

"Cool!" exclaimed Luke. "I am definitely going to like it here, so let's rock and roll!"

"Neat!" responded Laura. "Get some more sail on, Dad, and let's get going!"

"We are doing just fine. Be patient, and good morning, by the way."

"Oops! Sorry. Good morning, Mom, Dad," said Laura.

"Good morning, everybody," Adam, the eighteen year old, said yawning, the last one to come up on deck. He had stood the midnight to 4:00 am watch at the helm.

"Good morning, Adam," replied Sarah. "Come on, Laura. Let's go below and get breakfast on so we can be through and cleaned up before we drop anchor."

"With you, Mom."

Captain Dan McKay, USN, was happy. He sat back and sipped his coffee. *Here I am, nearing the end of my naval career with a dream assignment. It just doesn't get any better than this.*

When Admiral Winslow had approached him about the new duty assignment, Dan had not hesitated to accept it. Living in the tropics was a dream Sarah and he had shared since his cadet days in Pensacola, Florida, earning his Navy pilot's wings.

They had met at a social function at the naval air station and were married after Dan completed flight training.

One of their passions was sailing, so naturally they often shared thoughts of cruising the tropics and perhaps even living there.

In the years that followed, there was island life, but not the kind they often chatted about. Oahu, Guam and Japan were interesting in their way, but not like this was going to be. Those islands were just too large and too crowded to suit them.

Of course, there were Dan's tours of duty in Vietnam, which made this current assignment all the more appealing and in a sense, deserved.

The assignment offered was to supervise the clearing of an island in the Pacific Ocean on the extreme eastern edge of the Marshall Islands.

This island had been used by the US Navy for bombing practice in the 1940s and 1950s. In fact, so distant was this island from the nearest Marshall island neighbor that it had always been questionable whether or not it should even be considered a part of the Marshall Island group. After the clearing, Dan would remain as an overseer until an international court could decide what was to be done with the island, at which time the Navy would relinquish control.

The island, in shape a rough oval with an east-west axis of three miles and a width of about two miles, was dominated by an extinct volcano on the northeast that gradually tapered down toward the west where the land was quite flat. It was the flat western area that had been pummeled with bombs from ships and planes. Because the eastern part was unharmed and no threat to anyone, McKay had been allowed to bring his family with him.

They were approaching now on board the *Sarah*, a Pacific Seacraft model, the *Crealock 37*. The McKays were proud of her beautiful lines that turned heads wherever they were sailing. Dan had dropped in occasionally while it was being built on Orangethorpe Street in Fullerton, California. He loved to walk around its new oyster white hull with its blue trim stripes, admiring and appreciating the care that had gone into her construction.

Inside were six berths with Formica walls that contrasted with the abundant teak. Just to the left of the ladder leading below was a good-sized navigation table with Furuno radar, ICOM SSB and tuner, GPS, and a Yaesu FT-847 amateur radio installed above it. The galley sported a refrigerator with a freezer, microwave, two burner gimbaled stainless steel propane stove, and double stainless steel sink. The Kenwood stereo system did yeoman duty entertaining the twins. The Yanmar 4JH2E four cylinder, fifty-one horse diesel engine required little attention from Adam and Dan.

"The Admiral said that this north side was not as hospitable as the southeast side," commented Dan to Sarah, who had come back up topside with Dan's breakfast and hers.

"Well, yeah, there isn't much beach on this side, it doesn't look like," said Sarah, running her fingers through her short blond hair. "The volcano seems to climb almost straight up from the water, but there are lots of palm trees.

Boys, your breakfast is ready below."

They had now gotten close enough to see the coconut palm trees lining the north shore and the waves pounding the circling reef rather close to the shore.

Dan brought the *Sarah* a few degrees to port to skirt the island going from the north down past the east side, the windward side. As they neared the northeast coast of the island they observed a ridge curving out from the side of the volcano, running parallel with the volcano in a southerly direction. Vegetation on this "arm" prevented their seeing where the volcano met the water.

"We'll have to check that out when we have time," mused Dan.

"Yes, it looks kind of unusual, doesn't it?" asked Sarah.

"It certainly does. Very unusual, but possibly a good anchorage in bad weather."

At the end of the arm was an opening between it and the reef which encircled the island. Here they first saw how the volcano sloped down to almost level ground not far from the southeast shore and its ancient, rickety dock.

Just south of the dock, a Navy LCVP, a single-engine thirty-six foot boat with a hand-operated bow ramp, rested well up on the gently sloping beach. It contained supplies and household goods for the McKays. A jeep and an open utility trailer had already been offloaded onto the beach.

Dan gazed at his older son. Adam looked much

like his father, tall with dark hair and blue eyes. Also like his father, he tended to be introspective. *Looks like me twenty years ago....*

"Adam, go forward and see if it's deep enough here to let us get to the dock," ordered Dan.

"Okay, Dad," replied Adam as he moved to the bow and stared intently down into the clear water. "Looks okay so far."

Moments later, however, Adam called back to his dad, "The bottom is coming up now. Better hold up."

So with fifty yards to go to reach the dock, they dropped sail and a couple of anchors, and then flipped the rubber dinghy overboard. A few strokes with the oars put the McKays on the beach.

Dan stepped out and helped Sarah step ashore. Still holding hands, the family paused, as the kids joined the circle and bowed their heads as Dan offered a prayer of gratitude for a dream come true.

Chapter Two
Shaping Up

The channel through the reef and up to the dock was too shallow for the large offshore ships, so a dredge was waiting offshore to begin deepening the channel, after which the dock would be rebuilt and the Navy would offload the gear and supplies needed to accomplish the bomb clearing mission.

The plan called for the Navy's twenty-man crew to clear the island in two years.

The McKays, after briefly enjoying the view, began to organize the array of goods into some sort of logical sequence as the Navy lads packed the load onto the beach under coconut palm trees arching out toward the sea. Sarah and Dan were eager to get things stowed away, much to the disgust of Luke and Laura, who wanted to immediately explore, particularly the long-abandoned prison compound that Dan had described to them on the cruise down from Guam.

Adam would do as his parents directed.

The Navy jeep and small trailer would prove very valuable as the McKays gradually made trails wide enough to accommodate it. Being typical teenagers, the twins wanted to drive the jeep at every opportunity.

With the help of the jeep and trailer, they all began loading and hauling their things up a barely discernible trail to seven buildings arrayed in a semicircle around what had once been the administration building of the prison compound. As soon as the beach items were hauled and stacked against the outside wall of the large building, Sarah began to explore the buildings to decide where they might eat and sleep and decided they would have to sleep on the boat for this night.

At noon Sarah and Laura rowed the dingy to the *Sarah* and made sandwiches. Their first lunch was under the palm trees near the dock.

After lunch Dan and the boys began to reassemble Dan's pride and joy, the Piper J-3 Cub airplane. He had purchased it in Hawaii during an R and R break from the Vietnam War. A flying club based at Kipapa Gulch airstrip on the island of Oahu was disbanding, and a determined Dan had been the successful bidder.

First, they attached the wings, then by rigging a scaffolding that would lift the fuselage when the jeep pulled it erect, they attached the floats and propeller. Gasoline was added and an hour later the Cub was ready for flight.

A pole with a bit of ribbon on it indicated the wind was light from the east and blowing parallel to the south beach.

Dan climbed into the rear seat of the Cub's tandem cockpit, customary when flying solo, and buckled in. He paused to run his hands over the interior with a pleased sigh and then yelled, "Adam, get ready to start me."

"Okay. Switch off. Throttle closed."

"Switch off. Throttle closed."

Adam faced the propeller and carefully pulled it

counterclockwise a couple of times then called out, "Contact!"

"Contact!" barked Dan and flipped on the ignition switch, then inched the throttle forward slightly.

Adam gave the prop a hard spin, and the engine caught and roared to life. The sound was music to everyone's ears.

Adam and Luke, carefully avoiding the spinning prop, pushed the Cub's floats off the beach and turned it downwind. Standing in the water holding onto the floats, the boys hung on while Dan revved up the engine to check the ignition.

Dan gave the boys a thumbs-up and they released the floats.

Pushing the left rudder pedal all the way in, Dan moved the throttle on the left cockpit wall just below the window all the way forward. The blast of air struck the rudder and swung the Cub to the left, away from the beach; then he eased back on the throttle. Dan floated the plane downwind until the beach curved away from him, then swung the plane around into the wind and pushed the throttle wide open again. The Cub surged into the wind and soon powered past the family standing on the beach. When his speed was adequate he pulled gently back on the joystick and the Cub was airborne.

"Back in the air again. Yes! Love it!"

He slowly climbed to five hundred feet, then eased back on the throttle while pushing the joystick forward until he was flying straight and level. Everything seemed to be functioning perfectly, so he nosed the

Cub back down. A gentle turn brought him in line with the beach, which he paralleled at about thirty feet altitude.

The sun still shone strongly on the brilliant scene below; the pale blue of the shallow water, the whiteness of the sandy beach, the vibrant green of the palm trees arching over the beach dominated by the ancient volcano.

Awesome! Thank you God. We are so blessed! Guess I'd better land and take the others around to see a little of the island from the air. No, first I think I'll be a little selfish and fly up there and see what the crater of the volcano looks like.

Pushing the throttle forward to about eighty percent power and pulling the joystick toward him a few inches, Dan brought the nose of the Cub up a bit and began a gentle spiral upward until he was at nine hundred feet. As he flew over the lip, he throttled back, leveled off, and was pleased to see that there was a great deal of water in the crater basin. So much, surface area in fact, that he could have easily landed on it. This island was fortunate to have plenty of water, as many of the inhabited atolls of the Marshall Islands were experiencing serious water shortages.

That looks like about a quarter of a mile across, I'd say. This should meet our water needs for now. Back to the beach.

Dan flew out of the volcano's basin, closed the throttle, pulled the carburetor heat knob, and spiraled slowly down to the water near the waiting group, nudging the throttle occasionally to keep the carburetor clear.

He eased the nose up and touched down softly.

One by one, the McKays took their turn in the back seat with Dan in the front seat; as usual they wanted to fly it with Dad ready to take over in case of trouble. All their previous practices on Oahu were apparent. They were
getting so good on the Cub's controls that lately there had been nothing for him to do. Laura and her mother could handle the controls as well as the boys. Dan was pleased at how well his family had learned their ground and airborne lessons. The flight instruction had fit in nicely with Sarah's home-schooling.

Everyone enjoyed flying close to the volcano's water noting the vast volume it contained.

The water that overflowed from a lip in the crater cascaded down the mountain slope. Two waterfalls were evident; the first about halfway down the mountain slope, and the second near the base of the mountain where the water was captured in a pool. From there the flow meandered eastward to the beach, entering the water about a hundred yards north of the dock.

After the sightseeing was over, they hauled the bright yellow Cub up on the beach north of the dock and secured it to the trees so that a rising tide would not sweep it away.

"Let's go swimming," suggested Laura.

"You all go," Sarah replied. "I'll start supper."

After a mad scramble, they found their swimming togs and were soon enjoying the warm water.

About one hundred yards east of the dock was a small islet created when a strong current had managed to cut through the volcano arm.

"Let's swim over and check out that island," said Luke. They were all strong swimmers and covered the distance quickly.

As they walked ashore, Dan said, "Be careful and don't disturb anything here."

The small islet was a study in local flora. There was a profusion of various kinds of palm trees. Some of them were next to the water while others were higher up on the beach, creating little secluded beaches. Breadfruit trees dominated the interior. Dan thought he could detect a pattern in their distribution. *Related to the abandoned prison? Maybe.*

The highest point above sea level at high tide was a mere thirty feet.

A rapid walk about and through the islet revealed no particular point of interest until Luke let out a whoop.

"Over here. I've found a baby bird. Boy, is it hungry. Look! Its wing is broken."

The others hurried over to Luke and arrived just as he was reaching for the bird.

"Don't touch it!" ordered Dan firmly. "The mother will reject it if she smells your scent on it or so I have been told."

"I've heard that, but I didn't see any mother," reasoned Luke. "May I have it?"

"Don't be so impatient. Anyway, it's time to go. Your mother probably has supper ready. Tell you what.

Come back over here after supper, if it's not too late. If the bird is still hungry, then I'd say something has happened to its mother. If that's true, then you can take care of it. Deal?"

"Deal!"

The evening meal on board the Sarah was pleasant as usual, thanks to a portable gas-powered electric generator added at the last minute to run the refrigerator and freezer. This could not go on for too long because of the fuel consumption. Soon they would have to find another way to provide power and seek food sources.

They ate up on deck while enjoying a breathtaking sunset. The talk turned to the next day's plans, the ever-present subject of amateur radio, and Luke's bird, among other things.

"I'm going over and check on the bird. Laura, want to go with me?" asked Luke.

"Sure."

Soon they returned with the bird. It was extremely weak and could hardly hold its head up. Luke dripped some water down its throat then began to coax it to accept some shredded meat.

"Dad, can we work twenty meters after supper? That frequency band ought to be okay, huh? We could string a long wire to one of the trees and probably get out okay," began Laura.

"Well, it's quite a few feet from the boat here to that nearest tree, but give it a try," Dan said. "Keep an eye on the antenna. Be sure it doesn't sag into the water."

"Great!" Luke responded as he continued to feed his bird. It was soon full and content, so Sarah and Luke fashioned a splint for the broken wing, then placed it in one of Luke's shoes.

"What kind of bird is this?" asked Luke.

"Considering the shape of that beak, I'd say it was some kind of parrot, but I am no expert on birds," said Sarah.

"What about a name for this little rascal?" asked Laura.

"Well, that beak makes me think of that bird in the book Treasure Island. What was its name?" Luke inquired. "Remember? It was Long John Silver's bird."

"Cap'n Flint," replied Sarah.

"Hey, that's right, Mom!" exclaimed Luke. "Good job."

"Of course," laughed Sarah.

"Now, about tomorrow," said Dan. "Living on the boat is okay for a little while, but we need to get the large prison building shaped up for storage and get us inside. The rainy season will soon be here, so I want to be off the boat and in there while we are getting our house built. So, first thing in the morning we go up and get started."

"How about a picnic lunch up there at the lower waterfalls we saw when we were up in the Cub?" asked Laura. "Mom and I would fix it. Right, Mom?"

"Sounds good!" said Dan enthusiastically.

As it turned out, it was a good evening for amateur radio operating. Using Dan's call, N0AUZ, they were soon on the air.

After a couple of contacts with hams in the United States, they found themselves dealing with a clamorous "pile up"; many amateur radio operators all calling the one desired station at the same time as soon as a contact was completed. When the band began to fade away, the log of contacts made added up to forty-three. Twenty-one of them were from the states and the others from countries in almost every direction.

"Well, you never know when you fire up the rig and transmit *CQ, CQ, CQ, this is November Zero Alpha Uniform Zulu* what is going to be coming back at ya. Maybe we can go for it again tomorrow night," said Dan. "Tomorrow is going to be a hard day. Let's get some sleep."

"Roger that, sir!" replied Sarah smartly, with a laugh.

The gentle lapping of the waves upon the hull of the Sarah soon had them nodding.

Chapter Three
A Surprising Discovery

Everyone awoke early and had breakfast then Luke fed Cap'n Flint after which they all headed toward the prison compound. Since the materials they brought up yesterday were not stored in the large building, they could start cleanup immediately.

Dan issued orders rapidly. "Sarah and Luke, start removing debris. Tear away any rotten wood, vegetation, or the like and pile it outside. Adam, you and Laura take some buckets up to the waterfall and bring us back some water to scrub with."

"What are you going to do, Dad?" asked Laura.

"Oh, I thought I'd go take a ride in the Cub," he replied.

"What?" yelled Laura.

"Just kidding," Dan laughed. "Actually, after we have gotten started awhile, I'll go to work with the Navy crew, see how they are doing, and then be back for the picnic. Come on. Let's go up topside and tear into that roof."

"Right behind you, Captain, sir!" smiled Luke as he gave a goofy salute.

"All right," grinned Dan, giving Luke a shove toward the stairs.

They clambered up the rickety stairs to the top floor and stood gazing up at the brilliant blue sky above them. The roof had long since deteriorated and fallen to the floor.

"Pull down what little there is left then throw all this mess outside," directed Dan as he pointed to the large window on the south wall. "See you at noon."

Sarah and Luke attacked the mess and soon it was all lying outside. The blocks of the walls were still in good shape in spite of the years they had been there.

Adam and Laura returned after about twenty minutes with the water and carried it upstairs to begin scrubbing the walls.

Shortly before lunch time, Sarah said, " Come on, Laura, let's go fix the picnic lunch."

"Let's go," said Laura. She was glad to be away from the mess.

By noon the McKay boys had the upstairs clean and were waiting for Sarah and Laura to return with lunch. They didn't wait long.

"Okay, let's go eat. We'll start on the downstairs after lunch," said Sarah. So off they tromped up a faint trail through the vegetation. Soon it would be a well-worn trail. They had not been at the falls long before Dan arrived.

Luke and Laura spread a blanket in the shade of one of the many palm trees where they could sit and view "their" waterfalls, pool and the tropical vegetation.

"Looks like a travel poster," said Sarah. "It sort of reminds me of some of the scenes in South Pacific."

"It sure does," agreed Laura, raising her voice above the rumble of the falls, "I loved that movie and now it's like being in it."

Lush plant growth surrounded the basin that caught the falling water. The water rumbled as it hit the pool; they all had to raise their voices a bit. The volcano rose up from the picnic area like a giant bookend. The falling stream was about thirty feet wide as it entered the pool. The basin's bottom was shaped like a swimming pool; shallow away from the falls and getting deeper as it approached the falls. Under the falls, the water was about twenty feet deep.

"How is it going with the Navy lads?" asked Sarah.

"It's going well. They are getting organized quickly under Chief Daniels's direction."

"I figured that," she said smiling. "The chief is a super guy!"

"Yes, the men really respect him. They know about his service in Viet Nam."

After lunch Dan said, "Have you noticed that the stream running from here to the beach comes out just north of where the new dock will be?"

They had not.

"Well, I just learned this morning that there's going to be an oceanographic station built near there. The Admiral radioed Chief Daniels about it and gave us the job, with some help from the Navy boys. Do you think we can handle it? It will join the north end of the dock. The fresh water will be handy for lab use. It will be easier to distill than salt water."

"That's great, since we all have such a strong interest in oceanography," said Laura. "I can hardly wait. Wow! And yes, we can do it. Right, guys?"

"Right. Well, I am going to climb up by the waterfall and dive off those rocks," said Luke. He, like

Adam and Laura, was always dressed to go swimming.

"Let's check out the bottom first. I would hate for anyone to get hurt because we didn't check," said Dan.

So Adam and the twins waded into the warm crystal-clear water then each took a deep breath, swam down to the deep bottom, and thoroughly investigated for anything that could injure a diver.

When they popped back up, Luke said, "It's okay, Let's dive!"

He climbed up ten feet to a ledge, turned, and dove beautifully into the pool just in front of the falls.

Adam and Laura were on their way up to dive as Luke surfaced.

After several dives, Luke became bored and went exploring the far side of the waterfall.

After a couple of minutes, Adam asked, "Hey! Where is Luke?"

No one knew.

Just then Luke came into view from behind the west edge of the waterfall.

"Everybody come quick!" he yelled, waving them all toward him.

As they neared, he again boomed, "There is room to walk back here!"

Dan slid past Luke and followed the path behind the falling water. It was notched out of the face of the rock. At about the center of the falls, the path turned and led straight into the volcano. Almost immediately it was too dark to see.

"Go back!" shouted Dan above the roaring water

while motioning them.

They could not hear him but did as he motioned.

When they were far enough from the falls to be heard, Dan said, "Work until four o'clock, then we'll come back with some light and check this out. I should be back from the job by then."

"Okay. That's what we will do. Right, everybody?" said Sarah, looking at Luke.

"Oh, all right, Mom," mumbled Luke.

The afternoon passed slowly as they toiled at the cleanup. Luke checked on the bird occasionally as he had done all morning.

Dan returned before four o'clock, saw what they had accomplished, and said, "You've put in a good afternoon. Let's get some lights and go see what the deal is behind the falls. Luke, get a couple of lanterns and meet us at the falls."

"Yes, sir!"

Dan and the others had hardly gotten to the falls when Luke came running up to them.

"How's that for fast?" gasped Luke, holding up the lanterns in his hands.

"Adequate," laughed Adam.

So they reentered the tunnel with Dan in the lead. They had not gone far into the side of the volcano when the passageway narrowed to a hole just large enough for Adam, the largest in the family, to crawl through comfortably. As they emerged from the hole and stood erect, they observed a domed room about forty feet in diameter with a flat, pulverized volcanic rock floor.

Shining their lights around the room, they found nothing but a pool of water on the far side from the opening they had come through.

"Let's check the water. Is it fresh or salty?" asked Dan.

Adam knelt down and brought a handful to his lips.

"It's salty," he said as he directed his light into the pool. "It must have come from that hole I can see down there in the bottom."

"I wonder where that goes," murmured Laura pensively.

"Don't know. We can come up sometime and check on it with scuba gear on," replied Dan. "It's time for supper. Let's head out of here."

After leaving the waterfall and its noise, the youngster chattered about the discovery of the cave, then Dan mentioned some of the projects they had facing them.

"I hardly know which to do first. We've got to design a power system, build a house for us, a guest house, and the oceanographic lab with quarters for its personnel. Since the Navy has given me a budget to cover these, I think it is time to go to one of the nearer inhabited atolls and hire some help. I'm going to take Adam and sail to Ni, one of our neighbors to the west," said Dan. "I'd go in the Cub but the atoll is beyond the Cub's fuel range, and we couldn't bring anyone back with us that way anyway."

That evening, around a cozy fire on the beach, they ate and chatted again about the day's events until

they all began to feel drowsy. It had been a busy day.
So, off to bed they went.

Chapter Four
Meeting the Neighbors

It was still dark the next morning as Dan and Adam prepared to set sail.

"Sarah, we will be monitoring 7.260 megahertz in case you need to contact us. Give us a call from time to time. Got it?" said Dan.

"You bet," replied Sarah. "Now on your way and hurry back."

She cast off the lines to the boat as Adam pulled them in, coiled them neatly and secured them. The sails filled and *Sarah* began to surge forward.

"Perfect sailing weather, Dad," commented Adam as he came on deck a short time later with coffee and a hot roll right out of the microwave for each of them.

"Roger that. If the wind holds, we should be there by Sunday, since today is Wednesday. That's making about a hundred miles a day."

"Dad, you said yesterday that one thing we had to do right away was to get some permanent power generated. What are we going to do about that?"

"Well, I've thought of several things. Maybe use one of the waterfalls to power a hydroelectric generator. Maybe solar panels to charge up some large storage batteries or maybe wind power, since the wind blows steadily on the island. I've even thought about working with the oceanographers to use tidal power. Then I thought maybe we could eventually tie it all together in a power grid. We probably will go first with the hydroelectric power station and set it up by the upper waterfall. When we get back, I will see what the admiral thinks of it and if he would have a generator shipped in for us with their regular supply run. He will probably go along with it, since the Navy crew can use it also."

"Wow! That sounds great! I can't wait to get started. I like your ideas, Dad. Want me to spell you?"

"Sure. Hold her steady on the present heading of 285 degrees. Think I'll go below and see what's going on on the ham bands."

"Okay, Dad." *It feels so great to be out here aboard the Sarah. She's sailing beautifully. Just look at this ocean...a dark blue this time of day. And here comes another seabird by to check on me. Wow! It's hard to beat this.*

That night, as he stood the midnight to 4am watch, Adam marveled at how fast it passed. It was a moonless night and the stars were extremely bright. He gazed up and thought of the names of all the constellations visible to him that he had learned since he was a boy sailing with his dad. Because he had never been this far south, he was seeing some constellations for the first time. He had studied the star charts and knew where and what they should look like and there they were! Now added to star gazing was watching the manmade satellites passing through the sky. The International Space Station was gradually coming together and could easily be seen as it crossed the night sky not long after sundown, or right before sunrise. Now there was a permanent crew up there and an amateur radio station was installed and operating. Also, there were the mysterious ocean sounds just beyond his ability to see the source that rounded out the night.

The McKays would be contacting amateur radio satellites up there as well, when they had time to acquire the antennas, software, hardware, and interfacing for the computer to the radio. Of course, there was the GPS—the Global Positioning System using geostationary orbiting satellites to give a fix—but that would not talk back to you.

What moved time along quickly was ham radio. It was pleasant to talk to the family back on the island or chat with people from just about anywhere in the world while sitting out in the middle of a starry Pacific night.

At about 8:30 each night, in the Pacific time zone, they checked in with the Pacific Seafarers Net, a ham radio net on 14.313 megahertz that maintains contact with ships en route in the Pacific.

Each vessel gives her name, ham call sign, operator's name, position, destination, and any other pertinent data. It was nice to know that they were being kept track of by any number of hams listening in.

The second night was not smooth sailing, nor was the third. Rain and waves gave a "rocking horse" ride, but *Sarah* handled it beautifully.

The last night out was again smooth sailing.

They arrived at the reef of the small island of *Ni* around noon time.

"See a good opening in the reef anywhere?"

asked Dan.

Adam was looking through the binoculars. "Yes. I think just about ten degrees to starboard. Good navigating, Dad! We almost hit it right on the nose after four days of cruising."

"Well, we have done worse, haven't we? Get up to the bow. Keep me in the channel and away from the coral heads."

"Roger."

They entered the lagoon with no problem, dropped sail and anchored when the keel touched the sandy bottom of the beach nearest the atoll's village. His dad had not used the engine, noted Adam.

All the inhabitants, dressed in their Sunday best for church and framed by the coconut palms arching over their heads, were gathered on the beach to welcome them enthusiastically.

An older man greeted Dan and Adam as they stepped out of the dinghy.

"I am Jimata," he said. "I am the iroij, the chief. Welcome."

"Hello," said Dan, "Thank you for this welcome to your beautiful atoll."

"Come meet my people," said Jimata, smiling broadly. "We seldom have visitors."

The people of *Ni* flocked around Dan and Adam and escorted them to a large building, the focal point of their village.

Dan, Adam and Jimata sat together under a shady palm tree in front of the building.

"Jimata, we are from the island east of here that

you call *Emmo*, or *Forbidden*. We are doing a lot of work on the island and could use help from some of your people, if it would be okay."

"What kind of help?"

Dan then described the activity going on back there and the type of help that was needed. He continued to inform Jimata that those who came would be housed in one of the smaller buildings of the prison compound until a home was built.

That evening they were entertained in a manner much like a Hawaiian Luau. The young girls tried to impress Adam as they danced. He was charmed, but he also noted that one of them did not join the others; she just sat by the fire smiling at everyone.

"Who is that?" asked Adam of the native to his right.

"That is Kamlani," he replied. "She is unable to walk because of an accident on the outer reef that left her paralyzed from the waist down."

That's terrible. She is beautiful! And what a smile!

About halfway through the evening he managed to casually work his way over to where she sat.

"Hello," Adam said.

"Hello," she replied, as she looked up at him and smiled.

That smile! Wow! Dazzling!

"May I sit here?" he asked.

"Yes."

"Thanks. I'm Adam McKay."

"I know. I am Kamlani Ronamu."

Oh, my! What a voice!

"It is very beautiful here."

"I suppose so. I have not seen any other places."

"Would you like to?" he asked.

"Yes, but since I can no longer walk I think it would be impossible." She stated this matter-of-factly with no hint of self-pity.

"How long since your accident?"

"Almost a year."

"I'm sorry."

"It's okay. I have lots of friends, and my mother and father are great. I think my father would like to work for you. He wants to take me to see a doctor in Honolulu about my back. So he wants to make the money to take me. Do you think he can work on your island?"

"I don't know. I'll talk to my father and see what he says, okay?"

"*Kommol tata.* Thank you."

"How do you say, 'you're welcome'?" He asked.

"*Kin jouj*, opposite the name of your island, *Emmo*, which means forbidden."

"Then *Kin jouj*," replied Adam and would like to have said more, but did not. He also noted that one of the young men was lingering about, watching him intently. *The boyfriend?*

The meal and entertainment over, the chief and his men met with Dan and Adam. It was decided that one family would go work on McKay's island; more would come later when needed.

With Adam's urging, Dan asked for Kamlani's

family. It was agreed. The Ronamu family would join Adam and Dan for the trip back to *Emmo*. Unlike most of the families on *Ni*, Kamlani had no brothers or sisters.

After an evening of visiting their new friends, they departed early the next Monday morning.

The return trip was very pleasant as the McKays got to know the Ronamus. Makko, the father, was tall and muscular. In contrast, his wife, Sope, was slender and delicately featured.

They arrived back late the following Friday evening. The Ronamus were warmly welcomed by the waiting McKays and several of the Navy men who were becoming acquainted with the McKays.

Chapter Five
Laura and Luke's Cave Encounter

Luke, Sarah and Laura started working on the oceanographic laboratory when Dan and Adam sailed for *Ni*. Chief Daniels supervised them on the construction. He was impressed with how well Luke and the women were at handling the tools and the building demands.

The Navy dredge had made short work of deepening the channel alongside the dock, and with the help of the pile driver had constructed enough of the dock to allow the McKays to commit to the lab construction full time.

The pile driver had the pilings for the oceanographic station extending well above the height of those for the dock. These taller pilings served as the vertical members of the lab building.

At the end of their first work day, Sarah suggested Laura and Luke go swimming in the falls pool. They had put in a hard day.

After swimming and diving for a while, Luke said, "Let's get the scuba gear and go check out that hole at the bottom of the pool in the falls cave. Want to?"

"I don't think the folks would want us to do that."

"We'll be careful. It's no big deal," argued Luke.

"Well, okay, I guess," she said hesitantly.

So they went to the storage room in the administration building, grabbed their scuba gear and headed back to the falls. They immediately went in and stood by the pool, shining their diving lanterns down into the hole at the bottom.

"You stay up here and keep an eye on me," ordered Luke, "then maybe you can come down."

"No!" she snapped. "I'm going down, too."

"Oh, all right." Luke knew better than to argue with Laura. When she made up her mind, no one was likely to change it.

They adjusted their face masks, then stepped into the water and followed the light from their lanterns to the bottom of the pool. At the bottom, they directed their lights into the hole they had seen before.

They turned and looked at each other. The hole was a tunnel leading someplace, but they could not tell where.

Luke hand signaled for Laura to wait while he followed the tunnel.

Laura's response was vigorous. "No!"

So they both pressed straight forward through the tunnel for several hundred feet, until it began sharply twisting about.

Suddenly, Luke slammed backward into Laura and froze!

Peering over Luke's shoulder, Laura saw why.

There, just inches from their faces, was a vicious-looking creature, its mouth open wide, exposing razor-sharp teeth capable of shredding flesh; its features eerie and sinister compounded by the light.

"Morey eel!" she gasped around her mouthpiece.

At the sound of her muffled voice and the rush of escaping air, the eel moved tentatively toward Luke's lantern.

He carefully placed his light on a small outcropping in the side of the tunnel and started easing back against Laura. The motion caused the light to fall to the tunnel floor. The moray attacked it!

Slowly, they retreated into the darkness of the tunnel until they could no longer see the light from Luke's abandoned lantern which the eel was shaking ferociously. With Laura's light they quickly returned to the pool.

As they emerged from the water, Laura exclaimed, "Cool!"

"Cool?" said Luke. "Why, that rascal was big enough to do us both in. This tunnel is something else, huh?"

"Yeah, I thought we were about to the end of it when we met the eel. With that dude in there, I wonder if we will ever know where it ends."

"I don't know," said Luke. "Wait 'til Mom and Dad and Adam hear about this."

"Boy, will they be surprised. They may get on us about going without telling them though; you suppose?"

Minutes later....

"Don't you two ever pull a stunt like that again!" ordered Dan. "That eel could have killed you, and we would never have known what happened to you. Do I make myself clear?"

"Yes, Dad."

"Yes, Dad."

"Now, tell me more about it," he said grinning.

Laura and Luke recounted their experience.

"We have a mystery on our hands. We don't know where that tunnel empties out and how do we get by that eel?" said Dan. "No one goes back into that tunnel until we figure out what to do with the eel. Understood?"

All agreed.

"Now, I have some news. Admiral Winslow said the oceanographic team would be here before too long. So when they get here I bet that they'll know how to take care of the eel problem."

"Right, Dad," said Adam. "When will that be?"

"I told the admiral the dock would be finished in about a week. He said then that we should be expecting the oceanographic team soon after that."

"Great! Never a dull moment on this island, huh?" said Laura.

The Ronamu family had been housed in the prison dwelling closest to the east beach, although they were seldom in it as it was too confining. In time they would be out of it and in a dwelling built just the way they wanted it.

Luke's bird now sat on his shoulder whenever he came near it. "Cap" was growing, and the wing seemed to have healed nicely, but it had no inclination to fly other than a fluttering hop to a shoulder.

Chapter Six
Power

Finally, they started constructing the hydroelectric plant, hauling the parts to the site in the jeep and its trailer as far as they could go. This was no easy job for Dan, Makko and the boys. In fact, some of the sailors volunteered to help occasionally. After they drove up so far, they continued packing everything up a trail to the upper, narrower falls selected because it could exert greater force on the turbine blades. They used blocks from one of the prison buildings to house the generator, thus protecting the electrical parts from the rain. The rest of it could be under an open canopy.

The hardest part was positioning the turbine blades so that the water would strike them the most efficiently. A sluice gate was rigged to control the water falling on the turbine blades.

There were the usual cuts and bruises, but toward the end of the third week it was finished. That evening they all gathered for a little ceremony; the throwing of the switch.

"Ladies and gentlemen, it gives me great pleasure to bestow on our first lady of the island the honor of throwing the switch to our new power system. When she does so, the lights on the *Sarah* will light up!

My dear, if you please." Then Dan placed her hand on the switch.

"Here goes!" said Sarah and threw the switch. The lights in *Sarah* lit, illuminating the area all around. One more hurdle had been cleared.

They lit a fire on the beach and had a great time celebrating the new power source. Later that night after the Ronamus had gone back to their dwelling, the McKays sat by the fire's dying embers.

Dan said, "I thought tomorrow we would crank up the Cub and everyone could get some stick time in, okay?"

And for the first time, to everyone's amusement and astonishment, the bird said, "Okay?"

Everyone laughed until tears ran down their cheeks and their sides ached.

"Okay!" they enthusiastically agreed.

The bird strutted around wondering what all the ruckus was about.

When everyone had quieted down, Laura said, "Dad, could you and I fly out to the south and see what's that way? We could be airborne in that direction about an hour and a half and have enough fuel to get back. Maybe even land if we find something and look around a few minutes, if there is anything to see, then head back."

"I guess so, but I don't think there is much to look at, and it will knock the others out of getting to fly," said Dan.

"That's okay," said Luke. "Just remember whose turn is next."

"I guess the rest of us can survive without flying tomorrow," laughed Sarah.

"Thanks, Dad, Mom, Luke, Adam!" said Laura, giving each of her family a hug.

"We are a hugging family, aren't we," laughed

Adam.

"That, we are," agreed Sarah.

Chapter Seven
Weather

The next morning Dan and Laura arose before the others, had a hasty breakfast and headed toward the Cub tied up on the beach near the half-completed oceanographic building taking shape at the end of the new dock.

"Dad, it's a great-looking dock, isn't it," Laura exclaimed.

"That it is, and the lab looks great, also."

The dock was indeed more than adequate. Two hundred feet in length, it met the Navy's specifications for their future needs. With the channel now deep enough to accommodate a rather good-sized vessel, progress was being made.

Laura sat in the front seat of the Cub so Dan could spin the propeller and bring the airplane roaring to life. That accomplished, he then easily pushed it off the beach into the water. Laura headed it south out into the channel as Dan climbed into the back seat, not touching the joy stick.

"Okay," Dan said leaning forward so she could hear, "find us a good stretch into the wind and take us up."

"Roger that," replied Laura, shivering with excitement and trying not to grasp the joy stick too tightly.

She ran through the pre-flight check, noting that the rpm drops of the right and left "mags" of the ignition system were within the prescribed rpm limit. She worked the control surfaces and gave Dan a thumbs up.

"It's your plane. Let's go," Dan smiled, remembering how tense with excitement he had gotten when he first started learning to fly.

Laura applied full throttle, then, steering with the rudder pedals, aimed at a spot some distance ahead. When she felt the plane was up on the "step," and the speed was sufficient, she pulled back gently on the joystick and they were airborne!

She held the nose up at a fairly shallow angle until they were at five hundred feet, then she leveled off, eased back on the throttle, and headed for any possible sites to the south.

Turning in her seat, she looked back at her father for approval.

Dan gave her a nod that said, "Well done."

*****

Navy Hymn:

Lord, guard and guide the men who fly

Through the great spaces in the sky.

Be with them always in the air,

In dark'ning storms or sunlight fair.

O, Hear us when we lift our prayer,

For those in peril in the air.

*****

Chief Petty Officer Daniels walked up the path from the dock area to the McKay's quarters, knocked on the door frame, and called for Sarah.

"Good morning, Chief," said Sarah. "What can I do for you?"

"Good morning, Ma'am. Well, we noticed the Cub flying out this morning and thought you'd want to know that a storm is headed this way. Could build into a typhoon. Can you contact them?"

"Maybe," said Sarah, "if they have the two-meter handheld transceiver on and they have some altitude. The handheld works pretty much line-of-sight and is influenced by weather conditions, as you know. I'll try to contact them. Thanks, Chief. By the way, how much time do we have?"

"In about three or four hours we'll notice the winds picking up and the sea building," replied the chief. "Good luck. See you later."

"Okay," said Sarah as she spun around and hurried up to their ham radio shack, which was really just the corner of the room. Turning on the two-meter transceiver, she called, "NOAUZ, this is KB0FKI, over," No response. She tried again. Still no response.

Guess I'll wait a few minutes and try again.

After several more unsuccessful attempts, Sarah

decided to leave the radio on with the volume turned up to where she could hear it from a distance.

Meanwhile, Dan and Laura were fortunate to come upon an atoll just barely above sea level.

Laura made a low pass over the atoll's lagoon to be sure it was suitable for landing. Satisfied that everything was okay, she turned and looked back at her father for approval.

Dan's response was a thumbs-up.

Laura brought the Cub around, lined up her approach, brought the throttle back to idle, and descended to just above the water. Then slowly she brought the Cub's nose up, killing the airspeed. Unable to hold its altitude, the Cub gently contacted the water.

Dan reached forward and patted Laura on the back. "Nicely done," he said.

Laura grinned broadly, pleased because, of course, he was correct. She taxied the plane far enough up on the beach that it would not float away.

Dan observed, "We were lucky to find this atoll. I suspect that we're at low tide here. At high tide, this atoll would be nearly underwater and we might not have spotted it."

They had not been on the small atoll long when Dan sensed a change in the air and the sea.

"Laura, we need to get headed home. I think the weather is changing on us rather rapidly."

"Okay, Dad," replied Laura, and with one last look they climbed back into the Cub.

Soon they were airborne again, and as they passed through one thousand feet, Dan turned on the handheld transceiver, and called, "KBOFKI. This is NOAUZ. Do you copy?"

Immediately, there was a response.

"NOAUZ. This is KBOFKI. I've been trying to get you for quite awhile. We are in for a storm. Hurry back!" ordered Sarah.

"We are on our way. NOAUZ standing by."

"KBOFKI standing by."

Dan touched Laura on the shoulder and pointed ahead of them. A long, dark wall stretched low across the northeastern horizon.

Laura's eyes widened.

"Take the rpm's up close to redline. We have got to get going!" ordered Dan. The engine of the Cub went from a purr to a roar as they raced the storm to their island.

"It's a good thing we left when we did." shouted Laura over the noise and looked back at her dad.

Dan nodded affirmatively.

Just minutes before touchdown they felt the wind jostling the Cub.

Turning into the wind to land, Laura felt some strong gusts.

"Dad, do you want to take over?" she asked.

"No, I'll just stay close to the controls if you need help, but it's still all yours."

The landing was okay, considering the gusty wind.

When they got out of the plane, Dan laughed, "White knuckle time, huh, Laura?"

"Right. But I thought I did pretty good," she said

firmly.

"That you did," agreed Dan.

Sarah, Adam and Luke were waiting.

"You didn't have the radio on, did you?" accused Sarah.

"No, not for a while," admitted Dan. "But listen, everybody, we had better get ready for the storm."

"I think we better tie the Cub down at the end of the lab building," said Adam. "Hopefully it will give some protection."

"Agreed. Luke, run and get me some rope from the storeroom. The rest of you get everything loose into the administration building. Get Sope and Makko to help you. Tie down everything you can't get inside. Now. Chop-chop!" ordered Dan.

"Hey, I almost forgot. Adam, get up to the power plant and close the sluice gate so the increase in water won't tear it out."

"I'm on it, Dad," and he sprinted away.

When they had gone, Dan paused for a moment, watching the ominous clouds building. How many storms had he been through in his naval career? How many times had he seen the immovable move? Only in a typhoon!

Chapter Eight
Bracing for the Storm

As Dan scanned the area looking for anything else that needed to be done, Chief Daniels came hurrying up.

"Since we've got the channel dug up into the arm quite a ways, we're anchoring our ships up there; you better get your boat up there, too, if you can! You all are welcome aboard with us to ride it out if you like."

"Thanks, Chief, but I think we will be okay. Good luck."

"Good luck to you, Captain," replied the chief as he hurried away.

Luke returned with enough rope to tie the Cub down, facing into the wind. With the plane tied down as best they could, Dan yelled for Luke to run for the boat tied to the dock.

"Hurry! The wind is getting stronger. It's going to be tough getting to the anchorage without banging into something!"

Dan and Luke jumped onto the yacht, untied it and drifted with the wind toward safe anchorage. Using oars from the dinghy atop the yacht's cabin roof, they fended off all objects threatening damage until they got in among the Navy ships.

"It's getting crowded, Dad. Now what are you going to do?"

"I'm going to start the engine and slip us in behind that last ship up there," yelled Dan over the wind now moaning through the trees and around structures.

At the last moment, Dan pushed the idling engine into gear, spun the wheel hard to port, shut down the engine, and floated smoothly into the niche.

"Let's get anchored and tied down fast and get out of here," bellowed Dan.

Luke was scrambling with every bit of strength he had to get the boat secured so they could head back to the administration building.

Job finished, they dropped into the water and swam the thirty feet or so to shore. Already, small bits of debris were joining the wind as its fury continued to increase.

While Dan and Luke were attending the yacht, Sarah and the others were scurrying to prepare their quarters for the blow. They nailed plywood over the windows. With some effort they tugged the generator inside.

Debris slammed against the south side of the building.

"Where are they?" asked Sarah.

"Dad and Luke will be here soon," assured Adam.

"They better hurry," replied Sarah anxiously.

"You know, at first, I thought it would be exciting to be in a typhoon, but now that I sense its power, I'm afraid we could be hurt or worse," lamented Laura.

Minutes passed, then there was a banging on the north door.

Adam ran to the door and jerked it open.

"Made it!" gasped Dan as he literally fell through the doorway, half supporting Luke as he did so.

"What's the matter with Luke?" asked Sarah as Dan placed him down on the floor.

"Head wound. We got the boat tied down and headed this way. At first we made good time into the wind, but the last quarter of a mile was rough. We were dodging all kinds of stuff flying through the air. Luckily, nothing really large hit us, though we saw some pretty good sized pieces of debris sail by. About one hundred yards from here, we were actually pulling ourselves from one tree to another. We were lying almost flat on the ground trying to move forward. Just when we got here, a palm frond stem smacked Luke on the side of his head and gashed him as you can see."

"Wow!" exclaimed Laura. "That looks nasty."

Dan turned to Sarah. "We've got to stitch that wound closed. Better now than when he is fully alert and feeling the pain more! Laura, get the first aid kit."

She quickly complied.

Laura shuddered as Dan and Sarah cleaned the wound and Sarah stitched.

Luke never uttered a sound.

As they covered the wound, Dan said, "You are one tough kid, Son. I know that had to hurt."

Luke's reply was a faint grin, a thumbs-up gesture, and a firm, "Naw."

"I thought the tunnel behind the falls might be a good place to wait out the storm, but we could see the wind and rain were driving the falling water back against the face of the volcano. There was no way to get in behind the water," said Dan.

"Next time maybe we can get in there early enough to avoid getting blocked out," suggested Adam.

"Right," agreed Sarah, "but when this is over we better see what happened in there, if anything."

"Yes," said Dan, "and have supplies in there just for riding out storms or any other situation."

The wind continued to howl....

"How long is this going to go on?" queried Laura.

"Could be hours, could be days. I just don't know," said Dan, "but whatever it is, we'll make it. This old building has been through many a storm before."

Just moments after he said that, the new roof suddenly blew away! Now the sound was deafening!

"Did you do anything to protect the ham gear?" shouted Dan.

"Yes. I thought it might be a good idea, and I guess it was," yelled Sarah. "I brought it down here."

The storm pushed the plywood panels against the windows, threatening to force them into the building where the McKays and the Ronamus huddled in a corner.

Night fell. Time passed extremely slowly as the roaring and banging dulled their senses. Sometime just before dawn Laura suddenly sat up from her blanket on the floor.

"Listen! The wind is dying fast!"

They all sat up groggily.

"You're right," said Dan.

"I'm guessing that we are in the eye and this is not over," said Adam.

"I agree. Considering that the wind stayed pretty well from the south and that it stopped abruptly, I'd say this is the eye and we had better prepare for the other half. Good call, Adam. The volcano should block some of its power. I hope," said Dan. "Adam, you and Makko go check on the plane. Try to face it north. Luke, let's go check on the boat."

"What about the rest of us?" asked Laura.

"Look around the area here. See if there is anything that could be a threat when the wind comes hard from the north."

"Okay, Dad," said Laura.

"Sope, check on things in your house."

"Yes, Mr. McKay."

"All right, let's get to it then," said Dan, "and hurry. It won't stay calm like this for long."

When Adam arrived at the plane he was shocked by the devastation. Several trees were down flat, one of them lying across the Cub. The oceanographic lab had suffered superficial damage. The main structure was still intact.

"Oh, no!" Adam gasped and ran to the Cub. Ducking under the tree, he pulled the fronds covering the plane and saw to his relief that the lab had taken the brunt of the fall, holding the tree off the Cub. Tying the Cub down next to the lab had been a good idea. Except for some holes punched in the fabric, the plane was okay…so far.

"Well, there's nothing we can do about this mess right now, Makko. Maybe the tree will protect it from the north wind, or will the tree move and finish off the Cub? Hmm…oh, well, better get back."

Dan and Luke hurried past the falls on their way to the Sarah and noticed that the cave might be accessible if they needed it. When they arrived at the yacht they were relieved to find it was undamaged.

"Dad, do you think this arm curving around us from the volcano will be enough to protect the boat?" asked Luke.

"I really don't know, Son. I'm hoping so," sighed Dan. "Let's reconfigure these ropes and anchors for the north wind. Maybe next time we will go further up into the arm up there."

The job finished, they hustled back to the others.

"Sarah, Laura. Did you find any problems around here?" asked Dan.

"Well, maybe. Did you notice that some of the trees on the northwest corner here are leaning quite a bit?" asked Sarah.

"No, I didn't. If they have loosened up their grip on the soil they may flop over on the building when the wind picks up again," said Dan. "Let's go look, everybody, and see what we think."

Chapter Nine
To Storm Cave

As they came out of the building, Dan noticed the wind starting to gently move the trees on the eastern slope of the volcano. *Uh-oh. Here it comes*, he thought and looked at Makko, who saw it also and nodded.

"Oh, man!" said Dan as he looked at the conditions around them. "This is no good. Adam, run to the falls cave as fast as you can. See if we can get in there, and if the cave's okay!"

Adam was almost out of sight before Dan finished the order.

Minutes later Adam returned. "It's okay!" he gasped.

"Grab what you think we may need everybody and let's get moving!" shouted Dan as they all scurried to their quarters.

"Laura, get something to catch water from the falls in. I'll grab the rig. I don't want to leave it here." A strong gust of wind put emphasis to his words.

After grabbing the items, they ran hard for the cave with Adam carrying Kamlani, since he was the strongest.

Dan was the last one to step behind the waterfall. As he did so, he took one last look and was alarmed at how the wind had built since they left their quarters.

"Let's see if we can get this firewood burning," said Dan. "If there is no ventilation in here, we will soon know. Better keep it small in case we have to put it out."

Luke and Laura soon had a blaze that lit the cave, casting their dancing shadows on the wall.

"Look! The smoke is going out through that place up there on the wall," said Laura. "Guess we get to keep the fire, huh?"

"Funny," smirked Luke.

"Adam, thanks for bringing the firewood up here while Laura and I were flying. I didn't think we would need it so soon, but here we are," said Dan, his black hair still wet from the waterfall. He carefully placed the ham gear against the wall, out of their way.

"It's so quiet in here. Hard to believe what's going on outside," murmured Sarah.

"Makko," said Laura, "tell us about your island and your people."

So for some time, Makko stirred their imaginations with stories about his boyhood in the islands and atolls, until the fire burnt low. His voice broke with emotion as he described what happened to some of his relatives who were living on Bikini Atoll when the Navy relocated
them. It had been against the will of some of those who had an idea what was about to happen to their island; atomic testing. The Navy moved them to another island further away, which was not nearly as functional as their beloved Bikini home.

Then in a more cheerful mood, he explained his

fishing methods and how he would take friends and relatives fishing in the outrigger canoe that they had made together. He thoroughly explained his methods for crafting items from sharks' teeth, fish hooks from pearl shells, knives from seashells, hats from palm fronds. Accompanied by hand gestures, he explained how to use powdered palm bark to stop a bleeding wound, how to make sennit, or palm twine, which could hold a sixty pound tuna by rolling coconut fiber between the hand and thigh to a thickness of one eighth of an inch, and on and on.

    The McKays were fascinated with Makko's contribution to passing the time. As they sat around the fire listening to Makko, Adam's gaze frequently paused on Kamlani's lovely face. When their eyes met, her eyes would flick downward and she would shyly smile. Sarah noticed this and was pleased with her son's feelings toward the gentle Kamlani.

    Although they could barely hear the typhoon raging outside, there was evidence that nature was rampaging. The water level in the pool in the cave floor was bobbing steadily up and down; it came close to spilling out onto the cave floor occasionally.

    "I'm glad we are not in the tunnel down there today," said Laura, pointing down into the cave floor pool.

    "You've got that right, Little Sister," agreed Luke.

    "Quit calling me that, you big jerk. Cut it out!" ordered Laura, pushing Luke into the wall by the entrance to the cave.

    "Okay, okay," laughed Luke. "I'm quitting! I'm

quitting!" Then, as he moved away from the wall, he noticed that it felt wet behind him. "Hey, this wall is wet!"

Chapter Ten
A Mystery

Adam aimed his flashlight on the wall behind Luke.

"Look at that. There is water running down the wall. Where did that come from?"

The flashlight beam tracked the water up the wall to the hole where the fire's smoke was escaping.

"Well, it looks like another mystery to add to the list," said Dan.

Efforts to scale the wall and examine the source of the water at first were in vain. The water made the wall too slick to ascend, although there did seem to be some hand and footholds.

"We'll bring a ladder back when the storm is over and check it out," Dan said. "If we can get one in here."

"I'm gonna go see how it's doing outside, " said Luke. "Want to go with me, Laura?"

"Sure. Let's go," said Laura, and hurried to the tunnel ahead of Luke.

As they neared the waterfall, the roar of the falling water was thunderous. Water spilled over the lip of the crater above them at a tremendous rate.

"Crater must really be getting rained into!" yelled Luke in Laura's ear. "If that water touched us, it would probably slam us into the bottom of the pool."

So they returned to the cave and reported what

they had seen and heard.

"Well, we'll just have to wait until the water slows down," said Dan. "That could be a while."

"What if the food and firewood are used up?" asked Laura.

"Guess we'll figure that out when the time comes," replied Dan. "I don't think we will be here long enough for the food to be a problem, but the firewood is not going to last much longer, even if we keep just a small one going. Maybe we had better start making some plans."

It grew quiet in the cave, and after some time Adam sat up suddenly.

"I've got it!" snapped Adam. "Let's make a human ladder and see if we can get up to that hole."

"Yeah," said Luke. "Strongest on the bottom, then next strongest, and so on. so I guess it will be Adam, Dad, and then me on top."

"Okay," said Dan, "Let's try it."

Adam walked over to the wall below the hole, spread his feet wide, leaned slightly into the wall, spread his hands on the wall about the same as his feet, then braced
himself as Dan crawled up his back and stood on his shoulders.

"Good," said Luke, "Here, Kamlani, hold onto the bird. Here I come."

With much grunting and groaning, he made it to where his knees were on Dan's shoulders and his arms, chest and face were pressed tightly against the wet wall.

"If I can just stand up now, I'll be able to reach the hole," he panted, grimacing from the wound on the side of his head after he banged it against the wall.

"Hurry up!" growled Adam. "You all are really heavy on me down here."

"Okay, okay," said Luke as he slowly inched his way up the wall, the wound throbbing noticeably.

Finally, he was standing erect atop the human ladder. Reaching into the hole above his head, he felt what seemed to be a rod secure enough to support him.

"I've got hold of something up here. If I can get my other hand on it, I can pull myself up. Got it!"

With every bit of strength he had, Luke pulled himself up and over the lip of the hole.

"I made it!" he shouted. It looks like it goes 'bout thirty feet straight outward. I can see the clouds outside. Throw the flashlight up here."

This was quickly done, and as Luke flipped the flashlight on, he gasped! What he had thought was a rod was the upper leg bone of a skeleton sprawled at the entrance to the hole. The bone was lying across a notch at the bottom of the entrance hole.

"Whoa!" he shouted. "There's a skeleton up here!"

"Neat!" said Laura.

"Laura!" snapped Sarah.

"What else is up there?" asked Adam.

"Just this skeleton with... Wow! It's got a bayonet stuck in the base of its skull, and there's a pouch in one of its hands. Let's see.... It's empty! Here's a ring on one of its fingers. I'm going to check out the other end."

He walked through the tunnel bent at the waist. The opening was large enough that he could walk out, standing upright onto a projection much like a balcony in a theater. He eased out onto the projection far enough to see the pool below and got soaked in the process.

I can crawl down this slope when the wind dies I think.

Returning to those in the cave, he yelled down to them, "I can climb down the outside when the storm lets up. A tree fell over and caused some of the water to come into the cave up here. So, that's where the water came from on the wall down there. One mystery solved, another introduced."

"Okay. Be careful. Save your batteries," said Dan.

"Right."

Time passed slowly, but after waiting another four hours, Dan checked the tunnel entrance behind the falls and realized the storm was waning.

"We are going out now!" yelled Dan up to Luke.

"Okay. I'll try it from up here. It's pretty much daylight outside now. See you pretty soon."

Cautiously, they all exited their respective tunnels and met near the pool.

Luke explained the situation in the upper tunnel and showed them the items.

Dan examined the evidence and said, "Japanese military issue. World War II, but I don't know about this ring, nor do I have any idea about what was in the bag.

Another mystery. We seem to be getting our share of them!"

Chapter Eleven
The Aftermath

"Come on," urged Laura. "Let's get on down and see what the storm has done."

They moved slowly, picking their way through the snarled foliage and fallen trees until they arrived at the first of the smaller prison buildings. It still stood, but had been heavily damaged.

Makko's quarters, fortunately, was hardly effected. The north side of the administration building was caved in.

As they rounded its corner, Laura yelled, "Hey! Look down by the dock!"

Their boat had broken loose from its moorings and, dragging her anchors, had moved with the wind as far as the islet they had explored earlier. She was lying on her side.

They scattered, the Ronamus to their building, Sarah and Laura to the administration building, and Dan and the boys to check on the Cub and the *Sarah*.

The tip of one wing of the plane was all that was visible. Dan and the boys started throwing debris aside and soon Dan said, "Hold it! I think I can get in there and see if it's okay...yes! It's okay!"

"All right!" the boys yelled, high-fiving each other.

"Let's swim over to the boat," said Luke, "before she floats away."

So they did, stroking furiously.

The walked around her and found only minor

abrasions.

"Let's wait for the chief and the boys to get her back up on an even keel, then we will sail back up where we were anchored before until things get cleared up around the dock," said Dan.

The Navy obliged immediately and they were soon headed back up to the previous anchorage.

As they passed along the shore, Laura stepped out from the foliage and debris at the edge of the beach and gave them a thumbs-up.

Things must have survived, thought Dan, then he cupped his hands and yelled, "Go up and check the power station."

Laura nodded, gave another thumbs-up, and headed for the power station.

"Take her up as far as the water depth will allow," ordered Dan to Adam at the helm.

"Aye, Aye, sir!" barked Adam with a grin. He was so pleased with the condition of the Cub and the yacht that he just could not suppress his elation.

With just the engine and no sail, they eased close to the volcano until the keel gently touched the soft bottom and the boat stopped.

"Luke, tie a line to that tree off the bow," said Dan.

"Roger that, Captain, sir!" quipped Luke. He was also feeling pleased with the condition of things after the storm.

Chapter Twelve
Another Discovery!

Luke dropped into the water with the bow line, waded to shore and tied it to one of the undamaged trees. As he was doing this, he noticed a faint path leading around the curve in the beach. So while Dan and Adam were coming ashore, he followed the trail around the curve and stopped, amazed!

The volcano had a cave at its base! The entrance was almost covered by the storm tide.

"Hey! Dad, Adam. Hurry up! Look at this. There's a cave around here," shouted Luke.

Dan and Adam rushed to Luke and stood in wonder as the island continued to reveal herself to the McKays, little by little.

"Something else to check out after we get the mess cleaned up," said Dan.

"Well, let's get to it. I'm just itching to find out what this cave is all about!" urged Luke, leading the way as they hustled back to the others.

The administration building was badly damaged and would require considerable work to make it habitable again, if they should decide to do so. Their personal effects were mostly okay.

"We'll use the kitchen in the oceanography building as soon as we get it cleaned up and repaired, but until that's done, it's back to the boat again. We may have to give up on the admin building, but I don't know for sure yet. I guess we'll have to wait and see," said Dan.

"Now tell them about the volcano cave."

"Mom, you've got to see it!" said Luke. "It looks really neat."

"At low tide we will check it out," said Dan, "but after we get this all cleaned up, as I believe I said earlier."

"Great!" Luke growled. "This is going to take forever."

"Gripe, gripe, gripe," said Sarah, grinning because she knew that when it came to work, Luke would do his share along with a bit of good-natured complaining.

Between the McKays and Ronamus and the Navy, the clean up was accomplished, accompanied by a good deal of the expected griping by Laura and Luke. It was a long, boring week for all involved.

"I'm tired of this," said Luke. "I want to go check out that sea cave."

"Okay," agreed Dan. "I'm tired of this, too. Let's go."

So they all strolled to the sea cave. Kamlani went also, carried piggy-back by Adam, which suited both of them just fine.

They were fortunate that the tide was low at this time, and as they rounded the curve they paused.

There it was! The mouth of the cave was quite large. It arched out of the water and did not afford any means of entering other than by water.

"Why, you could taxi the Cub into there," said Laura.

"Yes, but as the water rises, what then?" replied Luke.

"Taxi it back out, I guess," laughed Laura. "Ha!"

"Funny."

Dan turned to Adam. "Go bring the dinghy here. We'll paddle in and see what we can find."

"Right, Dad."

When Adam returned, Dan and Luke got in with him and they rowed into the cave.

Chapter Thirteen
Yet Another Discovery

As they moved from the bright sunlight into the cave, they paused to allow their eyes to adjust.

"Look at the ceiling," noted Adam. "It's tall enough that when high tide almost covers the mouth of the cave, there is still lots of room overhead, maybe ten feet or so."

"Let's go in further," said Luke, as they sat in the middle of the cave looking around.

"Can't," said Adam. "We are hung up on something."

"Well, shine your light down and see what's going on," said Luke impatiently.

Adam directed the light's beam into the water under them. The water was quite clear and the thing that had snagged them was obvious to him immediately.

"There's a sub down there!"

"Sure there is," laughed Luke, thinking Adam was playing a joke on them.

"Here. See for yourself," replied Adam as he handed the light to Luke.

"Well, I'll be!" murmured Luke and handed the light to his dad.

"It looks like the two-man subs the Japanese used at Pearl Harbor in 1941," said Dan. "We could probably find out from our ham friends, but I'm pretty sure I'm right."

"Great!" said Luke. "Now, let's dive down and look it over."

"Wait a minute, Son," said Dan. "Let's look around with the light first. Who knows what might be lurking down there."

"Good idea," agreed Adam.

"'Good idea'," mimicked Luke sarcastically.

It was a good decision. The light revealed several places around the walls of the cavern that housed some vicious-looking Moray eels! Some were gigantic, as moray eels go.

"Excuse my smart mouth, Adam," said Luke. "You all were right. Well, we have got to do something about those eels."

"Apology accepted," replied Adam.

"No one goes into this water until the eels are cleared. Agreed?" asked Dan.

"Agreed!"

"The oceanography people will be here soon. Let's see what they suggest doing about them."

Sarah shuddered when they returned and told her about it.

"Oh, let me go see!" Laura pleaded.

"Not now," said Dan. "We have got to finish getting the oceanography lab ready for the oceanography group. By the way, I don't know about you all, but I'm getting tired of saying *oceanography* all the time. From now on it is the *O lab, O group,* and so on. Okay?"

"Okay!"

"Okay?" croaked Cap'n Flint. He was always good for a laugh, and they did.

That night, around a cozy fire on the beach, they discussed the day's events. After a time, Adam and Luke went to the ham rig, worked a couple of dozen "hams" before the band faded, and quit for the night.

Chapter Fourteen
The O Team

The O lab was housed in a building that included living quarters for the O staff. The McKays and the Ronamus had worked hard all week putting the finishing touches on it in readiness for the arrival of equipment and personnel.

Now as the boat bringing them neared the dock, Dan turned and looked one more time at their accomplishment. Although there was always more to be done, it was ready for occupancy.

Starting at the north end of the dock, the lab stretched along the beach for nearly forty-five feet to where the Cub had ridden out the storm.

A person could walk on the dock to the north end straight into the O lab and O team's living quarters.

"Welcome to Emmo, I'm Dan McKay,"

"Jim Conrad."

They shook hands vigorously followed by Dan introducing his family and the Ronoamus.

"Hello to you all, I'm Jim Conrad. This is my staff; Harry Townsend, physical oceanography; Susan Upchurch, biological oceanography; and Edward Toguchi, chemical oceanography."

Everyone shook hands around, then Dan said, "Okay, let's give them a chance to settle in. Come on, folks. I'll show you to your quarters."

Jim Conrad, a tall, powerfully built man, ducked slightly going through the doorway, then nodded approvingly.

"Looks good! Everything I asked for seems to be here," he said.

The other oceanographers agreed.

"I think you will like your quarters," Dan said. "Each room, as you can see, opens out onto a sun deck or lanai extending out over the water several feet."

"This is great!" exclaimed Susan. "I love it! I can work on my tan."

"Very nice," said Edward. Harry nodded agreement.

The individual rooms joined a long multipurpose room which would be their kitchen, conference room, library, or whatever else would be needed. The lab itself was located between the dock and the living quarters.

"We have been using the kitchen in the O building here until we get a more permanent place to live. The storm destroyed our quarters, so we have also been sleeping here since we got it cleaned up. Now that you all are here, we will move back on the Sarah until we can get the prison building ready to house us again. We're not going to do much to the admin building, just enough to protect us, then we start building a permanent home for whoever the future occupants happen to be after we leave. You can see the top of the main building from here. See?" asked Dan as he pointed out of the great room windows toward the prison compound.

They nodded.

"This is quite a place," said Susan, who, at twenty-five, was the youngest of the O team.

"More than you realize," Adam said.

"As I said before, let's give them a chance to settle in a little before we fill them in," suggested Dan.

"Okay, Dad," agreed Adam. "See you all at supper pretty soon."

"Right," said Jim Conrad. "See you in a few minutes."

The crew soon had their gear stowed away.

Supper was a great success. The McKays, the Ronamus and the scientists got acquainted quickly and were soon enjoying themselves thoroughly. The sub, of course, was a major topic of conversation. It also turned out that all the scientists, except Jim Conrad, had their ham licenses, so there was no shortage of stories that were shared.

The bird, which had now adopted Kamlani when Luke was busy, proved to be a source of entertainment as well. Its raucous *okay* created a good laugh for the O team.

Chapter Fifteen
The Moray Eel Problem

"Miss Upchurch, what can we do about the moray eels in the cave?" asked Laura. "We're anxious to get into the sub."

Susan, the biologist; an attractive, tanned, natural blonde, responded, "Please call me Susan, Laura. Now, since we seem to have room here, I suggest keeping some of them in tanks here at the O lab for observation until the sub is out and the cave has been searched. The rest I would say to remove to a safe distance away and turn them loose."

"Sounds good to me. Maybe there is an atoll around here," said Dan, "that is underwater at high tide so they would not be bothered much by people cruising around. Maybe the one that Laura and I flew to just before the storm. We'll have to check on that."

"Morays are shy unless provoked and they don't see very well, so I think we can catch them in a steel wire mesh trap if we can be patient in luring them out with some food they like," said Susan.

So it was decided that Jim would show Adam and Luke how to cut and weld the holding tanks and traps to the desired size; Dan, (when not with the Navy crew), Sarah, and Laura would work on the building of the McKay house; the Ronamus would assist on the McKay house, then start one of their own; and the O team would proceed with the organization of the lab and continue planning their research.

After the boys finished work on the trap, they then created holding tanks for the eels to be lodged along the bank north of the dock.

Work progressed smoothly with occasional breaks to enjoy the island and cruise around on the *Sarah* looking for a suitable atoll for the moray eels. Nothing suited their needs. As it turned out, the island that Dan and Laura had flown to was indeed quite adequate for the eels to thrive.

The day came when the McKay house was finally finished. It had rooms that surrounded a large room in the center of the house, the great room. They also had a door to the porch from each of the rooms. The porch completely surrounded the house.

Frequently, they all gathered in the great room of the McKay house and talked at length about each others plans, particularly on Sundays after an informal church service and meal.

Jim Conrad and the other scientists talked about their work and the projects they were hoping to implement, with the major goal being a thorough study of the island's coral ecosystem. The McKays were fascinated with his part in the search for the giant squid. Although the search had failed to view the squid in its natural environment deep down in the ocean depths, the attempt did not dampen, but actually increased, the expedition members' desire to try again later.

The McKays shared their hopes for alternate power sources to supplement the hydroelectric plant, a runway large enough to handle military aircraft, raising food for their needs, having livestock on the small islet across from the dock, a sturdy tower to support the beam antennas for the amateur radios, and rescuing the sub from the cave.

What was not voiced was the fact that none of the McKays wanted to think about having to leave when the Navy's job was finished and the island was turned over to some other authority.

The sub, oceanography and amateur radio dominated most of their conversations, as usual.

On this particular Sunday evening, Susan announced, "Everything is ready. Dan, if it's okay with you we'll start trapping Morays tomorrow. We'll need help, of course."

"You have it," said Dan.

Monday morning was beautiful. The sunrise was spectacular. A brief early morning shower had brightened everything. Everyone's spirit soared at the beginning of this perfect day.

The O crew and the McKay boys lugged the traps up to the jeep trailer and drove along the beach following a trail they had just finished, dropping the traps as close to the sea tunnel as they could get.

"Be careful putting these in the dinghy. It would be easy to punch a hole in it," cautioned Jim. "We can't all get in the dinghy, so we'll take turns. Susan will go each time with one of us until we have all had a shot at it. Okay, Susan?"

"Sounds good to me," she responded. "Come on, Eddie. Let's see if this is going to work."

As they entered the cave they noticed how quiet

it was. The water dripping from the oars was magnified by the acoustics of the cave. It was not difficult to maneuver around the sub. "Have you noticed how little wave action there is in here at the moment?" asked Edward in a hushed tone.

"Yes. That and the sound. It sounds like we are in a well," she agreed. "Dan says that it isn't always smooth like this. Sometimes there is a lot of swelling action. Well, let's ease this first trap down here just inside the cave mouth. Let it down until it rests on the floor."

"No problem."

Slowly, to avoid disturbing the Morays, the cage was lowered to the cave floor. It was designed to drop the trap door when the eel pulled at the bait at the far end from the door.

"I think this will work as soon as we find out what kind of bait they like and if they are hungry," said Susan.

The morning sun shone through the mouth of the cave and illuminated the cage.

Edward and Susan sat motionless for several minutes, then an eel shyly peeked out at the trap and the bait which swam back and forth in its small cage. The eel advanced as far as the opening to the cage, then darted back into its hole. This went on for some time. Each time the eel was bolder.

Susan noted the size of the moray. If it were longer than the trap, then it could back out when the door was dropped and escape capture. It was going to be close on this first one.

"Come on," She whispered. "Strike the bait."

Moments later, the eel glided from its lair straight to the bait, striking at it viciously. The door dropped and latched successfully.

They had captured their first moray eel.

"Yes!" said Susan softly as she raised a clenched fist. "We got lucky on the food choice, so now we know what they like to eat."

The eel was furious and thrashed violently about the cage, but the structure held.

"Okay," said Susan. "Let's take this rascal back to the holding tanks. Hang on to the rope while I row us out of here."

The eel renewed its fierce attack on the cage when it was lifted from the cave floor. It was all Edward could do to maintain his hold on the cage.

"Hurry!" pleaded Edward as the others approached the boat. "Grab the other ropes and give me a hand!"

The plan had been to row back to the tank, but that idea was abandoned as Susan was afraid the cage lines would puncture the rubber dinghy; thus, an awkward walk followed instead.

Fortunately, the sandy bottom along the beach was fairly even so after a twenty minute march they finally were able to hoist the cage over into the holding tank.

Susan released the latch and the eel quickly glided into a rocky crevice at the end of the tank where an eel habitat had been constructed.

Susan took each of the others into the cave to

have their turn at catching Morays. Each time, she waited for the uncaptured eels to settle down after the turmoil created by the previous one.

When all the eels had been trapped, the McKays borrowed the Navy's motor launch and towed the caged eels to their new home, the atoll to the south.

It had taken two days to capture the eels; seven of them in all.

Tuesday night, gathered around the campfire on the beach, they discussed the captures and made next day's plans...dealing with the sub.

Chapter Sixteen
Raising The Submarine

"Because the Navy's too occupied with its duties right now to assist us, it's up to us to salvage the sub," reported Dan. "They are, however, letting me use their motor launch again to pull the sub out of the cave and tow it down to the dock. "Adam, you and Luke dive down and check around. Be sure the sub is clear of obstructions, then we'll pull it out."

"Gotcha," said Luke as Adam and he quickly donned their scuba gear and disappeared under the water at the mouth of the cave.

The water was quite clear as they passed through the cave opening. They could see the bottom was flat and composed of ground up igneous rock and sand giving it a marbled, sandy like appearance.

Upon entering the cave they snapped on their lights then separated and slowly moved along the sides of the sub.

Everything was okay for towing. Adam noticed how good the hull looked, considering it had been there for so many years.

As they met at the rear of the sub, Luke noticed something lying in the sand just below a hole in the cave wall toward the back. It was the light he had left in the tunnel below the storm cave pool when Laura and he had to retreat from the Moray eel. Teeth marks were clearly visible on it.

How about that! Now I know where that tunnel

went. It empties in here. Wow!

Adam and Luke gave each other a thumbs-up then turned and swam back to the group waiting outside.

"The sub is okay to come out," said Luke, "and I found the light we left in the storm cave tunnel, Laura. Look at these teeth marks."

"Wow!" exclaimed Laura.

"That's what I said to myself," laughed Luke.

"Is there no end to the intrigue on this island?" asked Sarah.

"Doesn't seem to be, Mom," replied Adam. "I'd guess there's more with the sub coming out now."

"Yeah," said Luke. "We ain't seen nothing yet!"

"Okay, now boys, take these flotation devices in and place them so that we can inflate them and lift the sub off the cave floor," instructed Dan.

The devices were sets of bags with a wide strap between them. Bubbling air into the inverted bags using the Navy's air compressor causes them to rise to the surface and be able to support some of the sub's weight between them.

"I think six sets of them; three forward of the conning tower and three aft should do the trick."

It was a time-consuming job, but after a couple of hours the sub was suspended about two feet off the cave floor. It had been difficult getting the straps under the sub with it sitting on the cave floor.

Towing the sub to the dock went without mishap. The straps were hooked to the doc so the hatch would be available even at high tide. That accomplished they were ready to open the hatch on the conning tower of the sub.

"Well, it's not full of water," noted Dan. "or it would not have towed out so easily."

"Oh, you're so smart, Dad," smiled Laura.

"I know," replied Dan with an exaggerated air of superiority, then laughed. "If we can blow the ballast tanks, we can remove the straps and she should then float on her own.

The hatch refused to budge at first, then with the help of an eight-foot-long iron rod wedged in its spokes it yielded. Finally the hatch could be lifted.

"Stand back and hold your nose. This is probably going to smell bad," ordered Dan.

He opened the hatch.

Everyone immediately retreated from the sub's hatch area.

"Yuck! That smells terrible!" exclaimed Luke.

"Gag! I could just barf," commented Laura.

"Luke and Laura. Go get enough extension cords and a fan so we can blow that stale air out of there," said Dan.

"We're gone," replied Laura as they raced to the admin building.

When they returned, the fan was set on the edge of the hatch and aimed down into the sub's dark interior.

Toward evening the sub was aired out enough to be entered.

Dan climbed down the ladder, but reappeared immediately.

"Too dark. We need more light in there. Adam, go see what lights you can round up to string through down there."

Adam returned some time later with the needed string of lights.

"Got'em from the Navy," explained Adam as he plugged them in with the fan. "I'm glad we have hydroelectric power now, because this would make the generator pull hard." He checked the on/off switch. They worked fine.

"Here you go, Dad," said Adam, handing the lights to his father in the hatch.

Dan descended the ladder, stood on the control room deck, and switched on the lights.

"Uh, oh," he murmured. Looking up through the hatch, he yelled, "Adam, come down here!"

Adam climbed down the ladder and stood beside his father.

"Look."

Dan stepped aside to reveal a skeleton drawn up in the fetal position.

"Hmm. Looks like the captain went down with his ship, huh?" said Adam.

"Don't move it. We'll let Admiral Winslow take care of it."

"No problem there. Another mystery, huh?"

"That's affirmative," agreed Dan. "I'm going to contact the admiral. I'll be back soon. Let everyone have a look. Search the sub thoroughly, but don't take anything out of here until I get back.

Sarah, use the video camera to record the

corpse and the rest of the inside. Luke, run and get it."

He returned in short order.

After the initial surprise at seeing the skeleton, everyone bent at the waist to avoid bumping the overhead and walked one by one through most of the sub's seventy-eight foot length. Inside, not even the shortest of them could stand up straight.

It was Laura who found it.

She had reached in through a small opening under the navigation table and pulled out a rolled-up notebook that still held its shape, though the rubber band that once held it had long ago disintegrated. Sarah videotaped this discovery also.

Dan finally returned and Laura showed him where she had found the notebook.

He placed it on the navigation table. Everyone gathered around the hatch above him.

"Let's see what we have here."

Chapter Seventeen
Treasure

Very cautiously he unrolled the fragile notebook. Inside was a piece of tattered cloth holding six beautiful white pearls approximately three eighths of an inch in diameter and one large, magnificent black pearl an inch in diameter!

They all gasped as one when the pearls were revealed.

"Fantastic!" exclaimed Luke. "What are they worth, Dad? Are they ours?"

"Uh, well, I don't know. We will give them to the Admiral and see what the Navy says about it," answered Dan. "As for the value, I don't know, but I'd say they are quite valuable, especially the black one."

"Will the Navy give them back to us?" asked Laura.

"Don't know that either, but let's look at the notebook," said Dan. "Hmm...just as you might expect. It's written in Japanese."

"How do you suppose they got the pearls?" asked Sarah.

"I don't know that either. Maybe the notebook will have some answers for us."

Edward had been looking down from the "con" hatch above with the others and said, "I can read it. Hand it up here."

So in the gathering twilight Edward translated as

everyone gathered around him on the sub's topside.

"The notebook was the skeleton's personal diary. Much of it is unreadable," said Edward then continued.

"He was Ensign Shamata, captain of the submarine. His crewman was Petty Officer Second Class Yamoto. The diary chronicles Ensign Shamata's time with the sub from the premature separation from the mother sub long before their destination, Pearl Harbor, through their experiences in and around the island, to their being caught in the cave by a fallen tree during an earthquake. The tree had struck the sub's hatch so hard it could not be opened, thus trapping the two of them inside. They could retreat back into the cave, but other trees had blocked their attempt to exit from the cave.

Yamoto had tried to get out through one of the torpedo tubes.

One part of the diary is almost unreadable. In it, there are some vague references to pearls.

Ensign Shamata closed out the diary saying, 'Yamoto made it out because I could hear him trying to open the hatch, but he could not get it open. When I tried to escape, I was unable. Breathing very difficult now...lights fading...batteries dying. This will be my last entry. Farewell to my family...'"

"Read the part about the pearls again," requested Laura.

"It reads: 'As for the pearls, we found a...at...pla...and...brought...and put...in the sub. The others...second cave. Because the rad...working, we are unable...Navy but keep...they will find us soon. One of the natives...island west of here has...but we...him. We...black pearl and a few...hers here in the sub. The others are in cave located...from here.'"

"Poor man," murmured Sarah.

The hush that followed lasted for some time as each imagined how the sailor's last hours and minutes must have been. Why had he bothered to stick the diary back in its hiding place, and what about the native? Their reflection was finally ended by Luke.

"I wonder what happened to the other sailor and what other cave?"

"Well, we have the guy we found above the storm cave, but was he Japanese or the native? If he was not Japanese, then what was he doing with the uniform on and was he killed by the missing sailor?" asked Adam.

"It's just one mystery after another," commented Laura.

"That it is," agreed Sarah. The others nodded in agreement.

"I have had enough of this. I'm going swimming," announced Luke. "Anybody want to go?"

"Me," said Laura. "Wanna go, Kamlani?"

"Sure," she said, looking down at Adam, "if someone will carry me down to the water." She had remained on the dock rather than be carried onto the sub.

"No problem," Adam said. "I'll carry you."

I'll light the dock torches," said Dan. "You all go on."

"Thanks, Dad," said Luke and he turned and dove into the water on the side of the sub away from the dock.

Adam ascended the ladder to the dock. Gently, he picked Kamlani up in his arms, and as her arms encircled his neck he felt her breath on his neck and his heart beating hard in his chest.

I wonder if she can see me blushing and feel my heart beating?

He strode from the dock onto the beach, then into the water at the end of the O building.

Wish I didn't have to let go of her. What am I thinking? Careful, Adam boy.

In the water, Kamlani had no trouble getting around even though her legs were of no assistance.

The swimmers gathered under the Hawaiian-garden-style torches and were delighted to see that a great variety of fish were attracted to those lights.

"This is great," said Laura. "The fish, the perfect water, and look, a full moon is coming up. What a great night!"

"Enjoy it, "said Dan from the dock rail. "It doesn't get much better than this. Thank the Lord that we can all be here and share this moment."

After the swim, the O Team, Ronamus, and McKays gathered around a small fire on the beach before going to bed.

"Thanks for making this fire, Makko," said Adam.

"You're welcome. What's going to happen with the sub, Captain?" asked Makko.

"Well, Admiral Winslow said that after the Navy examines it and catalogs it, we can use it here around the island. If we can upgrade the batteries and maybe put up an array of solar panels to keep them charged when we are surfaced, then we could extend its range considerably. I think the O team will find it very useful in their work, particularly if viewing ports can be installed in the right places," said Dan.

"That would be a great asset to our program. We could pick a spot, submerge, then observe the organisms in their natural habitat," agreed Jim. "All the submersible research vessels that my boss has at his command are being used, so this is great!"

"I'll talk to the admiral to see if he will let me put some men on it," replied Dan.

"Has anyone thought about the other pearls? The diary said the other pearls were in the other cave. Is that the storm cave?" asked Sarah.

"Hey, that's right!" said Luke. "Let's go see if they are there!"

"It can wait until tomorrow," said Dan. "Goodnight, everybody. I'm going to bed."

So, many went to sleep that night thinking about the pearls. Adam thought about Kamlani.

Chapter Eighteen
The Other Cave

The next morning was beautiful on the Pacific island paradise. The temperature was mild. The swaying palm trees and the waves lapping gently on the beach gave Sarah immense pleasure and she again repeated as she so often did, "Thank you, Lord. We love it here...." Then she went in the house and put a Hawaiian music CD on the player and sat two of the speakers near the east and west doors. She turned the volume up to where the music could be heard some distance away from the house.

Ah yes. Love it!

After breakfast in the great room of the McKay home, the McKays, except for Dan, prepared to check the storm cave for the other the pearls.

Jim Conrad went with Dan to see about getting the sub modified for use by the McKays and the O team. The oceanographers busied themselves in the lab.

Adam and Luke took turns carrying Kamlani piggyback until they sat her down in the cave.

"All right, let's find those pearls," said Laura. Grabbing one of the shovels they had brought, she began to probe the floor of the storm cave.
Luke climbed up outside to what they were now calling Skeleton's Roost. Nothing.

Adam and Sarah carefully directed their lights on the walls and ceiling, but saw no evidence of a place to store anything.

Soon they gathered in the center of the cave and all said the same thing, no pearls.

"Luke, you and Laura get the scuba gear on and check the pool and the tunnel. Mom, Kamlani, and I will meet you at the mouth of the sub cave," said Adam.

"Okay, Big Bro!" said Luke. "Come on, Laura. Let's get moving!"

As Adam's group left the cave, Luke and Laura checked their equipment, then plunged into the pool. Soon they were at the bottom, and seeing no pearls after poking around, headed into the tunnel with Luke in the lead.

Slowly, they moved along, illuminating every irregularity of the tunnel walls. Again nothing but the sound of their breathing through the regulators and the air bubbles. Laura's regulator started malfunctioning slightly, so they returned to "Storm Cave" as it was now called, and corrected the problem on the way to join the others.

When they reassembled at the mouth of the sub cave, all were puzzled and disappointed that no pearls had been found.

As Laura and Luke sat on the beach with the others, Adam had a thought.

"You know one of the places we have not searched thoroughly is this sub cave. I know we saw a lot of it from the boat while we were trapping Morays, but we really haven't gone over the walls with the diving gear on, right?"

"Right!" said Luke. "Let's go!"

So they donned their scuba gear again and reentered the water. Luke moved along the left side and Laura took the right side.

Slowly they thoroughly examined the walls and met at the back of the cave. Again nothing.

Luke pointed up to the surface and they both slowly ascended.

"Rats! Looks like Adam was wrong. They are not in here," growled Luke.

"Well, let's go tell them," said Laura disgustedly.

As they turned on their backs and started kicking toward the cave entrance, their lights shone on the rough, irregular ceiling.

"Wait!" snapped Laura. "Look where my light is shining. Is that a hole?"

"What?" asked Luke, his light now also shining there.

"There it is, or is it? It goes up a little, then turns south. It could end right there, or does it?"

"I can't tell. Must be eight or ten feet up there from the water here. Let's go tell the others. Come on!" said Luke as he turned and swam furiously with Laura following.

"Did you find them?" Adam yelled at them from the bank.

"No," gasped Luke. "Not sure. Found something, but...."

Soon Luke and Laura were reporting what they had seen.

Laura asked, "How are we going to find out if it's a cave or not? It's way out of the water."

"We'll ask your dad. Let's head back now," said Sarah.

When Dan heard their results, he said, "Well, you were in there at low tide. High tide would have you much closer. Now, if the Japanese could position their sub so that the conning tower was directly under the possible cave, they might have been able to climb right in there." He reached in his pocket and pulled out a small book the Navy had supplied on the local tides. "It will be high tide at...1430 hours today, according to this. We will get the dinghy in there then and see what it is!"

"I'll go!" volunteered Laura.

"Sorry, my dear daughter, but it would be best if we put our tallest one up in there. That would be Luke," explained Dan, always impressed with his daughter's adventurous spirit.

"Yeah, Shorty!" said Luke, grinning mischievously.

Laura's answer to his sarcastic remark was a quick punch to his solar plexus, just above his stomach.

"Okay, okay," laughed Luke, holding up his hands in mock surrender.

"What about the sub modification, Dad?" asked Adam. "Are they going to do it?"

"Yes, they are. In fact, they have some men on it now," said Dan. "When they get through with it, it will be very useful to the O team and us."

"When will that be?" asked Luke, anxious to try it out.

"Probably about three weeks. It will be done

strictly voluntarily by the guys after they have finished their day's work."

"I can't hardly wait," said Laura excitedly. "It will be so great to sit in there and see all the undersea life of this area. Wow!"

"Can hardly you mean, Laura," corrected Sarah.

"Right you are, Mom," admitted Laura.

"The batteries to run the drive motors can be charged using solar panels when the boat is away from here. This can extend our range. The Japanese had only a hand-cranked charger, which took a long time to charge even one battery cell, and they had forty-eight battery cells to charge, thirty-six batteries in the aft battery room and twelve batteries in the forward battery room. The Navy is removing the original ones. They are a mess. They will be replaced with the latest power system we can find to drive the 600 horse electric engine and other power needs. For now we will be using some of the Navy's lead/acid batteries. There are more modifications that can be done in the future such as mechanical arms and the like, but they will have to wait. And, oh, yes, they are going to take several feet off the bow and just aft amidships to make it more maneuverable. Now, enough of my speech making. Let's get the dinghy up to the sea cave and see if we can get in that hole."

Soon Dan, Adam and Luke entered the cave in the dinghy.

Although Luke was supported by the others, he could not stand and touch the entrance to the hole, the dinghy was just too unstable in the flowing water and the ceiling too high to allow him to enter the opening, if it was one.

"Shine your light back as far as you can. See anything?" asked Dan.

"It turns south, but I cannot see far enough to know anything for sure," replied Luke. "Nuts!"

"Well, let's get out of here and think of something else," said Adam.

So they returned to the others with their results.

That night as the Ronamus, O team and McKays sat in the great room of the McKay house, it was decided that they would have to use the sub. Everything the Navy had was too large to enter the sea cave.

Thus, with days to wait for the sub to be ready for use, they all turned to accomplishing their various tasks and assignments.

Thanks to Makko and Sope, the new homes had a tropical design element; they were open to the air but could be closed if necessary.

When the finish work had been completed on the various buildings, the O crew started planning their research procedures using the sub.

The McKay and Ronamu families decided to take some time to get to know the rest of the island that was not a bomb hazard, so for a few days they traveled about the island in the jeep and the wagon pulled behind.. They agreed that one stretch along the south beach would be the place to build a runway for a fairly good-sized aircraft without destroying the beauty of the beach.

Another area paralleling the possible future

runway would be a likely place for a plantation. In its center was a knoll that afforded a beautiful ocean view to the south.

On the days that they explored the fairly flat parts, Luke, Adam and Laura loaded Kamlani in the jeep and took off. The undergrowth in some areas required slashing their way through for passage, but Adam and Luke did not mind. It was exciting for them as part of the island slowly revealed its beauty and potential.

Before the sub was ready for use, the explorable part of the island had been pretty well-covered, except for the steeper slopes of the volcano.

Trails that would eventually be roads were beginning to develop from all the meanderings.

Chapter Nineteen
The Church

Three weeks after turning the sub over to the Navy, on a Sunday morning as they were assembled in the McKay's great room for Sunday religious observances, they were again joined by several sailors and officers from the Navy contingent. As they finished singing the Navy Hymn, Dan realized that a church building would soon be a necessity. The great room was getting crowded. Although the Navy would soon be leaving, there would probably always be a fairly large number of people on the island at one time or another.

That evening, Dan voiced the idea of a church building; it was enthusiastically agreed to by the regular group that had made it a habit of coming together in the evening after work or leisure. They were all sitting on the lab balcony this particular evening. The sun had just gone done and the torches had been lit. It was a magic moment on this tropical paradise.

"Where should we build it?" asked Adam.

"I was thinking about having it up on the ridge toward the falls, but not so close that the noise from the falls would detract from the service or whatever was going on. The ocean view there would be spectacular!" offered Dan.

"Sounds great to me," agreed Sarah, giving Dan a hug. The others agreed with that suggestion.

"I think one like those we saw in Hawaii would

be good," said Laura.

"Yeah. They were beautiful; white, with a steeple, and lots of windows that could be opened up," said Luke.

"Well, then, let's start drawing a set of plans and get it going," said Dan. "I am going to count on Makko taking charge of this, as it should be made in the Marshall Island tradition. Okay, Makko? Kind of a blend of the one in Hawaii and the Marshall Island style."

"Okay?" growled Cap'n Flint.

"Yes. Yes. Okay!" said a smiling Makko.

"Tomorrow evening we will all go up to the ridge and lay it out. We'll start with a prayer that God will bless all our endeavors on this island that He has led us to. How does that sound?" asked Dan.

"Marvelous!" replied Sarah.

The next day, not only did the usual group gather at the site, but the Navy as well, even the ones that usually did not come to the Sunday service. A strong spirit of unity had been growing among this gathering as the months had passed. It was never more evident than at this moment as Dan asked for quiet.

As all turned to Dan, framed by the rays of the sun that had just sunk below the western horizon, he bowed his head and prayed a most heart-felt prayer. Another precious island moment. Thus the church had its beginning.

Chapter Twenty
Some Flying Surprises

The next day, as the usual group was having lunch together, Chief Daniels approached to let them know that the sub was ready for testing.

"We will tow it over here in the morning so you can look it over, then try its systems here close by the dock," he said.

"Good," said Dan. "I'll be over to thank the men personally after lunch."

"Okay. See you all. Bye," said Chief Daniels. With a salute to Dan which was returned, he was gone.

After the talk about the sub had settled down, Dan said, "Anybody want to take a ride in the Cub?"

Everyone wanted to go.

"It's my turn," said Luke, "but I see Kamlani wants to fly, so I'll take my turn later. In fact, I'll wait until another day because so many want to fly."

"That is so kind of you, Luke," said Sarah smiling proudly. "That's my boy!"

"So you want to fly, do you?" asked Dan, looking at Kamlani.

"Yes, I think so, maybe," she said hesitantly, looking at her father.

When he nodded his approval she clapped her hands.

"Thank you, Luke," she said and gave him a hug.

"You're welcome," said a blushing Luke.

"Okay, boys. I am going down to the work site for a few minutes so you can get the Cub in the water and lift Kamlani into the front seat."

"We're on it, Dad," said Luke. Minutes later they had carried her to the Cub. It was a little awkward, but they managed to get her into the front seat and strapped in securely. It was not long before Dan returned and plopped into the back seat. Everything checked okay, so with a wave to the crowd from Kamlani, they headed into the wind at full throttle.

Dan saw Kamlani tense up, so he leaned forward, patted her on the shoulder and raised his voice to be heard over the engine noise. "Relax. We are okay. Just relax and enjoy the ride."

She looked back at Dan and smiled.

What a lovely girl. No wonder Adam likes her so much. I guess we all do for that matter.

This was Kamlani's first flight and it seemed to her that the sea and the island were dropping down away from her as the Cub slowly climbed. At two thousand feet, Dan leveled off and circled the island.

"It looks so different up here. You can see everything, but it looks flat down there. Even the volcano," said Kamlani to Dan who was leaning forward to hear her.

Dan eased the stick forward and the throttle back, gently gliding down to just a bit above the volcano's crater. He then began to fly as close as he safely could to the areas they had not been able to show her from the ground.

She frequently turned and gave Dan an appreciative grin, pointing at various places she recognized and nodding.

After about thirty minutes of this sightseeing, Dan brought the Cub down to a perfect landing right in front of the others standing on the beach.

When Adam and Luke helped her out of the plane, she reached back, gave Dan's hand a squeeze, and said, "Thank you, Mr. McKay. That was wonderful!"

"My pleasure, Kamlani," replied Dan.

One by one the O crew took their turn in the Cub. Then, as the McKays took their turn with Luke going last, each flew the plane themselves from takeoff to landing. Finally, even Sope and Makko went up, after a lot of coaxing.

Then to everyone's surprise and amazement, Dan said, "Sarah, this would be a nice day for your first solo, don't you think?"

Sarah and the others were stunned. There had been no discussion of this. Before she knew it, Sarah found herself strapped into the back seat and looking forward at the empty front seat. She was alone in the Cub!

"Just take off, circle out south where we can see you, then bring it back in, okay?"

"Okay!" replied Sarah with a look of anticipation.

She had flown the Cub so much since their arrival, that she was feeling quite confident.

As Sarah taxied out and turned into the wind, Adam said, "Are you sure she's ready, Dad?"

"Yes. I'm sure. Just watch her," said Dan, staring at the

plane as it gathered speed and gracefully lifted off the water.

Sarah flew as she was instructed and came around for the landing. As the plane came close to the water, the McKays unconsciously drew closer to each other.

The landing was nicely executed, to everyone's relief.

Everyone was jumping about and yelling as Sarah nosed the Cub up on the beach, everyone except Kamlani, who was clapping and yelling.

Sarah was grinning broadly as she climbed out of the plane and into the cheering crowd.

"That was fantastic!" gushed Sarah. "I'm glad you did it like that, Dan. If I had to think about it for a while, I don't think I would have done so well. I was up there thinking, well, girl, you got this up here by yourself and you're the only one that's going to get it down."

"And you sure did, Mom. That landing was a grease job," stated Luke.

"Of course," laughed Sarah.

Then to top it off, Dan turned to his family and said, "Who's next?"

Two hours later all the McKays had flown their first solo!

That night as they all sat about in the great room of the McKay home, they relived their experiences of the day. Then the talk turned to the sub again.

"It has been a good day. Tomorrow we check out the sub, so let's all get some sleep," said Sarah. There were no arguments. Everyone went their separate way thinking that it really had been a good day.

    Before Sarah drifted off to sleep, she prayed a prayer of thanks for this man that God had given her. Life was so good.

Chapter Twenty-one
The Sub Trial

The McKays had been waiting at the dock for about half an hour before the Navy launch finally came around the curve of the beach, towing the sub.

For the next hour the sailors showed the McKays what they had learned about the operation of the vessel.

The addition of viewing ports along the sides of the sub had required the re-routing of cables, pipes and the like. Particularly since several feet had been removed from its length. This was all quite professionally accomplished.

Dan was pleased with what they had crafted in such a relatively short time.

"Dad, couldn't we use the sub antenna for use with the two-meter handheld radio as long as it was above water?" asked Adam.

"Possibly," answered Dan. "We'll have to check the SWRs I expect. I think we have a simple tuner in the 'junk box'. Wanna go look and see?"

"Sure," replied Adam. "I'll be right back!" He hustled up the conning tower ladder, then up the dock ladder to the dock. From there he trotted up to the administration warehouse, soon found the needed items and returned to the dock, leaving the handheld radio with Luke.

It took only a moment to attach the antenna tuner and SWR meter to the two-meter mobile unit in the sub, adjust the tuner until it read close to a "one to one" reading on the SWR meter, and they were ready to operate.

Adam keyed the mike and called,"KB0OJT, this is KB0FKI . Copy, Luke?"

Immediately he heard, "KB0FKI, this is KB0OJT. Solid copy, Adam. Full quieting. No problem."

"Roger that. Thanks. KB0OJT this is KB0FKI. I'm clear and standing by."

Since the island was out of radio range for the two-meter radios to reach very far, they could have dispensed with using proper radio procedures, but Dan had said that they would do it by the book and so it was, most of the time.

"Okay, let's check this sub out," said Dan. "Adam goes with me. Luke and Laura get the scuba gear on and follow us down. Sarah, standby with the radio."

"Gotcha, Dad," said Laura.

The Navy launch slowly eased the sub away from the dock about a hundred feet to the deepest part of the dredged channel and stopped. Then the towing cable was removed.

"On this first dive we will just submerge enough to cover the conning tower. Here we go," said Dan. "Adam, dog the con hatch when you get inside."

"Aye, sir!"

When Adam was inside and the hatch was sealed, Dan directed him to slowly turn the valves that would allow the sub to sink. As he did so, the sub gently submerged until he shut the valves on Dan's order.

Dan and Adam looked out of the large port and starboard port holes. There was Laura on the port side and Luke on the starboard side. Each gave a thumbs-up when they saw Dan and Adam at the viewing ports.

"Okay. Now let's get the electric motor going and try moving forward slowly," said Dan, pushing a button on the control panel.

"We're moving," said Adam. "It's quieter than I thought it would be."

"Yes. The Navy added insulation here and there, which reduced the noise considerably," replied Dan. "Now I'm going to stop our forward motion and try reverse."

It went smoothly.

The check-off list that Dan had compiled all went well. The sub was ready for use; cautious use. More testing at greater depths would come later, but for now this was adequate.

When the sub emerged and made its way to the dock, Chief Daniels was there waiting for them.

"How did it go, sir?"

"Perfect, Chief! Your men did a tremendous job. I noted a number of modifications that you all did to it."

"Good. But I'm here because Admiral Winslow wants to see you over at our quarters."

"Be right there," said Dan. Turning to his family he said, "When I get back, we will take the sub up to the cave and see if we can get in that hole in the ceiling."

"We'll be waiting," said Laura.

Chapter Twenty-two
The Offer

Minutes later Dan marched into the Navy's temporary camp office a few hundred yards southwest of the dock along the beach.

"Hello, Captain, have a seat," said Admiral Winslow returning Dan's salute. "Looks like the Navy's job is moving along nicely here."

"Good morning, Admiral. I saw the PBY land down here in the lagoon and thought it might be you aboard. And yes, there's still much left to do. It is a slow process and fortunately we have had no one seriously injured. So, what's going on?"

"Well, I may have some good news for you. The jurisdictional court has decided that if you should happen to be interested in the purchase of this island they will sell it to you for one million two hundred fifty thousand dollars. The money would be distributed among the inhabited atolls according to population. You would have sixty days to come up with the money. What do you think of that?"

"Unbelievable! That sure seems like a small price for so much, but I don't know how we would come up with the money!" exclaimed Dan.

"I thought that was a generous offer, too. But this may help, the pearls are yours," the Admiral said with a broad grin. "There is more. Makko Ronamu is to have part possession of the island and is to select a number of families that would be willing to relocate from his home island to this one."

"These terms are all quite agreeable. God is sure remembering the McKays and the Ronamus!" laughed Dan. "I just can hardly believe it! Wait until I tell our families!"

"Now, this is with the further agreement that you will cooperate with the Navy in the future if they should have need of some of your island resources or facilities and for the oceanographic station to remain in service," said Winslow.

"No problem with that. You know that, Admiral Winslow," replied Dan as he stood and saluted smartly. "Thank you, sir. Thank you very much."

"Dismissed."

***

"...so that's the situation. My family will put our share of the pearls into purchasing the island. Makko, you all will pay a part that we can agree upon later," said Dan to the usual group gathered in the great room of the McKay's home. "I think that it is great that your family will be co-owners with us. You have been here with us almost from the beginning, and since it could be considered a distant part of the Marshall Islands, I am pleased that we can share ownership with you. I hope Kamlani will be able to have surgery to get her up on her feet again.

There is just one problem. The pearls we have right now will not even come close to being worth enough to cover the price of the island. So, it looks like buying the island and having the surgery hinges on our finding those other pearls, if there are any and if they are worth much and if there are very many of them. Even then we may be short and have to come up with a plan of some kind. Like getting a loan from some institution, maybe."

"Thank you, Mr. McKay. We will do our best to make this island a place we can all be proud of," said Makko, beaming broadly.

"No thanks needed, and I am sure you will do as you say. You all already are. Now let's take the sub up to the cave and check out that hole."

"All right!" said Laura, clapping her hands once, smartly.

Chapter Twenty-three
Pearl Cave?

Dan and Adam manned the sub and slowly headed to the cave. When they arrived, they swung her to starboard so that she was lined up aft with the mouth of the cave. Very slowly, Dan eased the sub backward into the mouth of the cave as Adam shouted directions from the conning tower. When they were under the hole, they studied the situation.

"This is not going to happen right now, Adam. The swells are too strong," said Dan then spoke into his handheld. "We are coming out, Luke."

"Roger," said Luke into his handheld. "What's the problem?"

"Too much wave swell. Adam could almost get into the hole at the top of a swell, but was five feet below it at the bottom of the swell. Too risky. We'll try again tomorrow."

"Too bad," said Luke. "KB00JT clear."

"NOAUZ clear," responded Dan.

"Dad, I've been thinking. What about using a grappling hook with some loops in the line like stirrups and see what happens?" suggested Adam. "If it catches good, we are in. Getting out is easy. Just drop into the water if necessary."

"Sounds good. I'll go down now and have Chief Daniels get me one made up for tomorrow morning. The timing of the throw must be just right to get it to go into the hidden part of the hole."

"Piece of cake," bragged Luke.

"We'll see," laughed Dan. "Now turn on the HF rig. Maybe we will hear from Hong Kong again tonight. If so, maybe we can get addresses of reputable pearl dealers or anyone who can get us in contact with them. I'll be back pretty soon."

"I'm on it," said Laura. "I'm going to get Kamlani. She wants to know more about ham radio. I'll let you know if I make a decent contact."

When he returned an hour later, Laura gave Dan an address that she had gotten from a school teacher in Hong Kong. Laura had aided Kamlani through a couple of the contacts. One was in Taiwan and the other in the state of Missouri. The Missouri contact was with a man who taught GED classes in one of the state prisons and had been stationed at NAS Barber's Point, Hawaii when Dan had been assigned there. He was a most interesting man who accepted an invitation to possibly visit the island when he retired.

"Dad, you might want to see if you can contact the man in Missouri. He was stationed in Hawaii in the same squadron that you were," said Laura.

"VW-14?"

"Yes."

"Small world, huh?" said Dan. "Yes, I'll give it a try tomorrow night."

That night everyone went to bed anxious for the next day and re-entry into sub cave.

Early the next morning Dan rose, made coffee, sat out on the porch, and began answering some correspondence that he had been putting off. That done, he sat back sipping his coffee and savoring the moment as he gazed about. The day birds were starting their daily business. The rising sun felt warm and pleasant on his face.

What a way to start a day! I must fly these letters over to the atoll where the mail boat stops. Maybe I'll have something to add to it if we can get into the sub cave hole. No, I better fly over this morning. High tide is several hours away.

Chief Daniels arrived with the Navy crew's mail and the grappling hook, so all they needed was a favorable tide.

"I'm taking the mail over to meet the mail boat," said Dan. "Who wants to go?"

Everybody wanted to go!

"Well, whose turn is it?"

"It's Luke's," admitted Laura. "Lucky dog!"

"Thanks!" said Luke with a grin. "I'm ready, Dad."

Soon they were airborne with Luke at the controls circling at five hundred feet and waving at the group below on the beach.

"Take us up to five thousand feet on a heading of 270 degrees. We should be able to see the atoll we're going to in about an hour at that altitude," said Dan.

"Okay," said Luke as he eased the joystick back a little more, increased throttle, and watched the altimeter slowly wind clockwise toward the 5000-foot mark.

At five thousand feet he leveled the Cub and

held their course on the 270 degree compass heading. The air was rather quiet, so the ride was smooth. Sure enough, about an hour after they were airborne, there it was, straight ahead on the horizon.

"Got it!" boomed Luke over his shoulder.

"Okay, now start a slow descent so that the plane's nose stays right on a spot you pick. Use the throttle, not the stick, to keep it there. It's good practice."

"So we maintain airspeed but are slowly sinking, right?"

"That's the idea," replied Dan. "Reduces fuel consumption."

Minutes later they neared the island.

"Circle the atoll and check for a good stretch of water where we can land into the wind," advised Dan.

"All right," answered Luke and he gently moved the controls so that he flew at 200 feet parallel with the beach on his left. He scanned the water intently for signs of any obstruction that could strike the plane's floats as he made a complete counterclockwise circle of the atoll. Satisfied with his choice, he lined up on his selected stretch of water and made a very nice landing.

"Nice job, Son," said Dan, slapping Luke on the back.

"Thanks, Dad," said Luke as he headed directly for the beach after the landing and eased up onto the sand.

After a brief visit with the local people, they delivered their mail to the one responsible for the mail and received some that had been waiting for them and the Navy. Soon they were airborne again.

"Dad, how come we went to Ni instead of this island?"

"Well, Chief Daniels told me some time ago that these natives had been having some kind of sickness in their population that had resulted in a number of deaths, so we went to Ni instead."

"Yeah, that makes sense, but I just had not thought of it before."

The flight back was pleasant and uneventful, and Luke again executed a nice landing.

When they had tied the plane down, Dan said to Luke, "I don't know why I bothered to go. You did a good job."

"Thanks again, Dad," said Luke, giving his dad a hug and a pat on the back.

"Well, by the time we eat lunch, it will be time to go try the sub cave again," commented Dan.

"Yeah, I'm ready," replied Luke.

Everyone was anxious to find out what was up there in the roof of the sub cave.

A half hour before high tide, Dan and Adam maneuvered into position under the hole and waited for the tide to lift them up to it.

"The swells are not as bad today," noted Adam.

"Right. Looks good."

Finally the moment arrived for them to try entering the mysterious hole.

"Adam, be careful when you throw the hook. You don't want it to come back and hit you," warned Dan.

"I know, Dad," said Adam, a bit irritated that his

father would think him that careless.

At high tide, Adam could stand on the edge of the hatch and touch the cave ceiling, but it was three feet further up to the possible crawl space.

Getting the grappling hook in where it would catch was going to take skill, timing and luck because of the up and down movement of the sub.

"Here goes," Adam called down to Dan.

The throw entered the passageway but did not hook on any surface, so when Adam pulled on it to test it, it came down toward him. He avoided it easily, but it loudly clanged against the side of the sub. Surprisingly, the next attempt caught and held.

"Got it, Dad!" yelled Adam triumphantly. "I'm going up now."

When the others knew he had gotten the hook to catch, they rowed the dingy into the cave.

Chapter Twenty-four
Pearl Cave Revealed?

Adam slung the light's strap over his shoulder and climbed with difficulty into the darkness of the hole using the stirrups. Yes, it was a hole, but how deep? He braced himself against the wall to regain his breath while shining the light around.

A space large enough for him to crawl through ran almost straight and level south, then curved downward. With a great effort he pushed off the wall and into the tunnel. He proceeded down the passageway, pushing aside a dense mass of spider webs. *Yuck!*

Cautiously, he aimed the light down into a larger opening. It had a floor. He carefully slid down into the larger space. Now he could stand. Quickly he flashed the light in a fast scan around the room.

Whoa! What was that? An old box. Hmm. Could this be it? Why else would a box be here?

He shone the light into it.

It was no false alarm!

"Wow! There must be hundreds of them in here!" he remarked aloud, his voice echoing strangely.

Running his hands through the pearls, he felt a large object in the middle of them. He pulled it out into the lantern's beam. It was wrapped in paper.

He unwrapped it carefully and there it was, a beautiful white pearl even larger than the black pearl!

This alone must be worth a fortune!

Adam laughed, carefully placed the large pearl back in the paper and buttoned it into his shirt pocket.

The metal box, about a foot square at the ends and two feet long with handles on both ends, had not rusted enough to allow the pearls to spill out.

When Adam lifted it, he was surprised at its weight. He was able to get it up into the passageway and squeeze past it. Then he drug it to the entrance where the sub awaited him and possible pearls.

"I got them, Dad!" he yelled down. "Great gobs of them. Be careful when I hand the box down to you. It's heavy."

As the box came into view everybody cheered wildly!

"We'll have to time it carefully," said Dan. "We must make the move at the top of the swell."

"Right."

Adam braced himself against the side of the hole and with a firm grip on the handle, slowly lowered the box toward his father.

After riding the swell up to the box several times, Dan finally grabbed the handle on the end toward him and yelled, "Got it!"

Adam released his hold on the box, and Dan lowered it to rest balanced on the edge of the conning tower before the sub reached the bottom of the swell. "Made it!" exalted Dan. "Now come on down."

"On my way," replied Adam, who neatly dropped onto the sub as it reached the top of the next swell.

"Now back to the house and let's see what we

have here!" ordered Dan as they emerged from the cave.

Soon they were all gathered in the McKay home around the table in the great room impatiently waiting for Dan to open the container.

Slowly, he released the latch and raised the lid. There was a collective gasp as they had their first look at the contents of the treasure chest.

Sarah spread a cloth out on the table and Dan carefully scooped out handful after handful after handful of pearls until they were all heaped on the tablecloth.

"We're all rich!" boomed Luke.

"You are right there," agreed Dan. "Now, if it's okay with you all, I'm going to arrange to meet the pearl buyers so they can bid on our pearls, okay?"

"Okay!" barked Cap.

"It may be quite a while before that happens, but we have
plenty to do in the meantime. Right?"

"Yes!" all agreed as one.

Savoring the moment, Adam said, "Wait a minute. Just one more thing," and stepping back from the group, he reached into his pocket, pulled out the paper and its contents, and set it on the table. He agonizingly, slowly opened it and revealed the large white pearl!

They stared at the pearl, speechless. Then there was pandemonium as they all, except for Kamlani, danced around Adam, hugging him and yelling. He then went to Kamlani so she could hug him also. Precious moment....

When calm returned, Dan said, "All right then. As I said, it will take some time to make the contacts and arrangements. I'll start as soon as I hear from the Hong Kong contact. I have a scheduled time to meet with her tonight on 14.250 megahertz on the HF radio. Right, Laura?"

"Right, Dad."

"Wait! There's something written on the wrapping paper," exclaimed Sarah. "It's a note. Here, Dan. Read this."

Dan took the note and looked at it. "I can't read it. It's written in Japanese. Here, Edward. What does this say?" and thrust it into Edward's hands.

Chapter Twenty-five
One Mystery Solved

"Well, this answers the question of who that body was that Luke found. The note was written by the other Japanese sailor. He states that the native had stolen the white pearl and the sailor's ring. The sailor followed the native to the upper cave and jumped him there. He got the pearl back, but could not get his ring off the body's finger. He was going to cut the finger off, but decided not to do so."

"So, another mystery solved," said Luke. "So what is the island going to hit us with next?"

"Good question...now I must hustle down to let the chief know what's going on so he can relay our findings to the admiral, and also to work out the time for Kamlani's operation."

Sope, who seldom spoke, just said, "Oh, my," over and over, with tears running down her cheeks.

Kamlani reached up and pulled Dan to her and gave him a hug.

The ham contact with the teacher went well.

Life finally settled down again. With the exception of an occasional rain, every day was a pleasant, sunny routine in paradise.

While they waited for pearl buyers and the operation date, work was completed on the O lab and the houses.

Chapter Twenty-six
Thanksgiving

Now it was Thanksgiving with turkey and all the usual accompanying trimmings. Considerable effort had been made to get everything to the island. The closest turkey had been in Majuro. The McKays had taken some time off and sailed to Majuro to get the supplies. Because their yacht had a refrigerator/freezer they were able to transport it back home without spoiling.

It was a pleasant trip. The weather held steady and was perfect for sailing. They all had their turn at sailing, navigating, cooking and relaxing under the tropical sun.

On the return trip, they were accompanied by a half dozen
dolphins that swam effortlessly just inches from the bow of the boat.

It was a great family time.

Upon their return, the meal was prepared by the ladies, who had a great time together doing it!

As they sat around the plank table in the McKay's great room, Dan offered a prayer of thanksgiving which went on for some time because there was so much for which to be thankful. He spoke eloquently about the beautiful island, how they and the Ronamu family were going to be able to purchase it, God willing, and the operation that was to occur soon for Kamlani, also God willing.

After the meal, the men took their coffee and sat out on the lanai on the side toward the dock. In their opinion, never had there ever been a more memorable Thanksgiving.

They sat there quietly enjoying the view of the beach and surroundings. Then they began to discuss all that had happened since arriving on the island some nine months ago. It truly was a time for thanksgiving.

The Navy had made great progress. Now there was a deep channel past the new dock and up some distance into the volcano's arm. The systematic elimination of unexploded munitions was progressing nicely. They were clearing from the south beach inward and had safely cleared five hundred yards into the island's interior all along the island's perimeter to where the volcano's ridge became steep on the south and west sides. Flags of various colors marked the progress. Detonations at first had been startling, but now they were hardly attracting any attention.

The power needs were met to some extent with the hydroelectric generation, but other energy sources would be needed in the future.

Now the O team members were beginning their mission work, about to utilize the sub.

"I'm sure glad we have the sub to use," said Jim Conrad. "It is going to eliminate a lot of our scuba diving which, of course, will save a lot of time and effort. Now we don't have to wait for the small research vessel that they are planning to bring us. It will work better than this sub, but for now we can get the show on the road."

Chapter Twenty-seven
The O Team and the Sub

Further trials with the sub by the McKays and the O team went well, and all were pleased with its performance. It was definitely going to be of great service to them.

One evening soon after Thanksgiving, Jim Conrad announced that the O team would like to take the sub out and start examining the coral formations in the reef around the island. This was, of course, decided at the time most of the decisions were made, when they were gathered in one of the great rooms. This time it was in the O lab.

"We want to take our time and carefully map out all the flora and fauna around this reef with particular attention to the health of the coral, then start branching out in ever-widening circles with this island at the center of what will eventually be a very extensive study of this particular latitude and longitude. If any of you want to go along, you would be very welcome. The more eyes the better," reported Jim. "Anyone interested?"

"Are you kidding?" asked Luke. "I am ready right now!"

"Me, too!" Laura replied.

"If it's okay with your folks, it's okay with me. Dan? Sarah?"

"I guess it's okay, if you obey Jim's orders to the letter. Understood?" asked Dan.

"Sure!"

"Of course!"

"Then so be it," said Dan. "Next time out, two more will go. We will have to work out some kind of schedule for anyone interested in going."

"All right, then. We meet at the sub at ten in the morning," said Jim. "No use going too early. Visibility will be best during midday. Again it has been another nice day in paradise. See you in the morning. Good night, everybody." With that, everyone headed for home.

Laura and Luke were so excited about the next day's prospects they found it dificult to sleep, but they finally did.

The next morning the twins were down at the sub early, quietly waiting for the O team. They sat on the dock watching the fish flitting about in the water under them. There seemed to be no end to the combination of shapes and colors.

Finally the O team appeared.

"You guys ready to go?" asked Jim.

"You bet!" beamed Laura.

"Roger that!" replied Luke.

"Okay, then let's get down there. Remove the power cord out of the hatch, Edward. Luke, cast off the lines," ordered Jim as the crew trooped down the plank to the sub.

"Aye, sir!" responded Luke. Edward just grinned at Luke and Laura's enthusiasm as he removed the power cord and secured it to the dock. The twins quickly descended into the sub.

"I thought it would be cool in here, but it isn't,"

commented Laura.

"No, the metal hull matches the temperature of the water it is submerged in," explained Jim. "It will get cooler in here as we go deeper, but not too much because we won't go deeper than the coral. Usually that is about two hundred feet. Coral only grows as deep as the sunlight will penetrate and where there is ample oxygen. Even in clear water that is about at the one-hundred-thirty-foot depth.

"Laura, do you remember the order of the colors of the rainbow?" asked Harry Townsend.

"Sure. I remember it by saying, 'Roy G. Biv.' Red, orange, yellow, green, blue, indigo, violet," Laura said rapidly.

"Very good. Well, some colors can go deeper than others. Red color is the first to be absorbed as the sunlight enters the water. If you were to scuba dive to one hundred feet and cut your finger, it would not bleed red! It would appear to be black!"

"Cool!" commented Laura.

"Neat!" Luke replied.

As they chatted, Jim Conrad headed the sub toward the opening in the channel between the arm coming down from the sub cave and the small islet across from the dock.

When the sub was far enough past the reef to submerge, Jim ordered the hatch closed.

"Stand by to dive," he ordered and all complied by grasping a handhold. "Down we go!"

As the sub tilted its nose down slightly and the water rose above the viewing ports, Luke said, "Look down. You can see the bottom dropping away. Boy, is this water clear!"

"We are going to slowly circle the island clockwise at a depth of fifty feet. If we see anything unusual, we will stop and shoot it with the camcorder. Also, we can mark the spot on the chart and perhaps scuba dive on it later for a closer look," explained Jim.

"The fish out here are different than those inside the reef," Laura noted.

"Right you are," said Susan. "Different environment, different organisms."

As they glided along smoothly, they talked about the pearls the Japanese had found and agreed they were probably from around the island somewhere.

The view through the portals was glorious. Schools of brightly colored fish passed into view, to the delight of those in the sub. Not only were the colors brilliant, but the shapes were also extremely variable. Then, to rival the fish was the endless panorama of the living coral beds. The variety even surprised Susan, who had researched coral in many parts of the world's oceans.

"Uh-oh," murmured Susan. "Hold up, Jim. Look at the coral here. See those patches where there is no coral? A starfish called *Crown of Thorns* did that. One of them can destroy as much as fifty-four square feet of coral in a year. Look! There's one...and there...and there! That's not good. We have got to do something about this!"

"Look at all those spikes!" exclaimed Luke. "That sure is a good name for them."

"Yuck! How do you get rid of them?" asked Laura.

"There is research going on to find ways to eliminate this threat, but right now we are losing ground in this world-wide battle. Anyway, one way is to use a hypodermic needle with a concentrated solution of copper sulphate in it. That would only help a little, as the oceans are so large it would be impossible to shoot all of them to the point of keeping them in check."

Jim, the sub captain for the day, eased the sub along at two knots.

"At this speed, we will circle the island in about three and a half hours," he commented.

"Good deal," replied Luke...then, "Hey, look out this side...the...uh...port side. A large sea turtle. What kind is it, Susan?"

"There are several kinds in this part of the Pacific. This one is the green sea turtle," she replied.

"The water is so clear it looks like the turtle is flying," observed Laura.

"Wow! It does look like that," exclaimed Luke.

As they cruised along, Susan shared some of her knowledge of the plants and animals of the sea. Laura and Luke were amused when she pointed out that many of what appeared to be plants were actually animals and what appeared to be animals, occasionally, were really plants. Camouflage in this water world was, indeed, carried to extremes. She also noted that there were a few oysters that might contain pearls.

About a third of the way along the north side of

the island they came to the mouth of a bay.

"I remember seeing this bay from the air," said Luke. "Remember this when you all were up?"

"Sure. I'd say everybody did," commented Laura. "Looks like a good place for houses."

Susan said, "Look. There is a great increase in the number of oysters on either side of the entrance."

"So, let's call it Oyster Bay," said Laura.

"Sounds good to me," agreed Luke.

So it was that the bay was henceforth referred to as Oyster Bay. It would remain to be seen whether it was aptly named or not.

Chapter Twenty-eight
What's That?

The cruise went smoothly for quite some time, then, as the sub rounded the volcano on the north, Edward said, "What is that on that shelf down below us? Stop, Jim!"

Jim did as requested and as he reversed the sub to where Edward thought he saw something, Edward said, "There it is in the shadow of the volcano. Hand me the binoculars, please. Hmm...looks like a ship to me. What do you think, Jim?" he asked as he handed the binoculars to the skipper.

Jim viewed the area in question and said, "Hmm...might be. Plot that on your map, Susan."

"Wow! Another mystery," said Luke. "How far down from the surface would you say it is? Could we reach it scuba diving?"

"I would say around sixty feet," replied Jim, "What do you all think, O team?"

They agreed with Jim's estimate.

"We could dive on it then! Wait until Mom and Dad hear this!" exclaimed Laura.

"Yeah. Wahoo!" whooped Luke, as the O team grinned at his enthusiasm.

The remainder of the cruise was uneventful, and the twins were anxious to see their parents to share their experiences of the day.

Later, as they were again with their parents, they did, indeed, share their experiences.

"...so we named it Oyster Bay, but the big thing was the possible sunken ship. It was hard to tell what shape it is in because there is a lot of stuff growing on it. Can we go scuba diving on it, Dad? Can we?" asked Luke.

"All in good time," replied Dan. "It must have sunk after the Japanese died, or they would have seen it, I imagine. Or did they? Much of the diary was unreadable so maybe...?"

"Hey, that's right, Dad," agreed Luke. "So...when do we go?"

"Tomorrow is Saturday, Dad," said Laura. "How about tomorrow?"

"Sure, why not, I am just as anxious to check it out as you all are," agreed Dan. "So, we'll go out there in the dinghy just before noon, when the sun will penetrate down there the strongest, and see what we can find out. Okay?"

"All right!" exclaimed Laura. "How about you O team guys? You want to go, too?"

"Not tomorrow," said Jim. "We will still be debriefing this little cruise we had today. A later day would be better for the O crew. Besides, you can't put many in the dinghy with all the scuba gear along."

To make the time pass faster the next day, the McKays all took a turn flying the Cub around and over the island, getting another look at Oyster Bay. From the dark blue of the water, it appeared that fairly good-sized yachts could enter and get rather close to the shore all along the edge of the bay.

Finally, Dan decided it was time to go check out

the underwater mystery.

With Sarah and Laura on the shore near the dive spot, Dan and the boys rowed the dinghy over the spot and prepared to dive. Luke was to stay with the dinghy while Dan and Adam dove.

Over the side and down they went. Because the mystery vessel was not in the volcano's shadow at this time of day, it was immediately obvious to both the divers that it was not a boat.

Well, I'll be, thought Adam, *It's an airplane...the wings are gone!*

Dan and Adam turned and looked at each other as they both realized what they were seeing. When they were down close to it, Dan recognized it as a pre-war Japanese transport plane.

So, thought Dan, *they did know the plane was here, but we could not tell because of the missing parts in the sub log. Hmm...*

Dan hand-signaled Adam that they would circle around the craft to look it over.

Adam gave his dad a thumbs-up and they proceeded.

The cause of the crash was not visible. The fuselage seemed not to have any major structural damage. The impact had caused the door on the pilot's side to be forced open and many of the windows were missing.

Dan approached the open door and cautiously peered inside. His light revealed a shambles. The impact had thrown much of the interior forward. Creatures of the sea now occupied much of the inside surfaces as their home. The plane was an ideal environment for a large variety of plants and animals.

As Dan's upper body entered the plane, he sensed a movement out of the corner of his eye. He retreated and shone his light in the direction of the movement.

Oh, my...!

It was a Moray eel larger than any of those they had removed from the sea cave. He turned and motioned for Adam to surface.

As their heads emerged from the water, Dan removed his mouthpiece and said, "Adam, there is an eel in there larger than any in the sea cave. We have got to get him away from there before we can search the plane."

Luke helped them into the dinghy as Adam shared what they had learned. "...and it is bigger than any of those we took out of the sea cave."

"Oh, man! So what do we do, Dad?"

"I think we will trap it like we did the others, since we already have a trap to use."

"Sounds good to me. Let's go get the trap and get to it."

"That's what I thought you would say," laughed Dan.

The trap was brought on site quickly, and soon they were again poised above the plane.

"My turn, Dad?" asked Luke.

"Roger."

Down they went and easily positioned the trap and anchored it to a seat frame as it was practically weightless in the water. After Luke examined the outside of the plane and peered in some of the windows, they returned to the surface.

"I didn't see the Moray," said Luke. "Suppose it is still there?"

"I'd say so," replied Dan. "It's a great environment for a Moray eel."

"Now what?" asked Luke.

"I am going to try to find out where the plane came from. I noticed a number on its vertical stabilizer."

That night Dan turned on the HF transceiver at the time that contact was usually made with Nancy in Hong Kong and called, "VS6XYL, VS6XYL, VS6XYL this is NOAUZ. Do you copy, Nancy? Over."

"NOAUZ, this is VS6XYL. Hi, Dan. I just turned on the rig and there you were. How is everyone? Over."

VS6XYL, this is NOAUZ returning. Hi, Nancy. You have a great signal coming in to the island tonight. How are you copying me? Over."

"Solid copy, Dan. What do you know? Over."

"Believe it or not, we have another little adventure going. We spotted a crashed plane in the water northeast of the volcano that we told you about. It is in about fifty feet of water. I was wondering if you could do us another favor."

Dan then explained that he needed to see if Nancy could get any leads on what plane it might be and any story that might have been published in the news about it and gave her the number on the fuselage.

"Wow! You guys have all the fun. Sure, I will get right on it and see what I can find out. May take some time. Let's keep our schedule again tomorrow night. I will let you know if I have made any progress, okay? Over."

"Fine, Nancy. That would be great! Good luck, and we will be calling tomorrow night, then." With that, they closed their contact.

Of course, when Dan cleared with Nancy, a great number of ham operators tried to make contact with him and the "pileup" lasted until conditions on the band got so poor that he finally said to those that could hear him that he was quitting for the night. By then, Sarah and the kids had gone to bed.

Another interesting day in paradise, he thought, as he yawned and also headed for bed. *I think I have made a mistake in giving out the info to Nancy over the radio. Lots of hams copied that. Be more careful Old Man!*

Chapter Twenty-nine
Solving another Moray Problem

The next morning, Dan dove on the wreck with Laura. She also took a tour of the outside. As she was doing so, Dan checked the trap. It had been tripped and the bait was gone, but the Moray was not in it!

Hmm, the cage is too small for this rascal!

Dan showed Laura the empty cage when she finished her circuit, pulled it out of the wreck and then pointed up. Up they went. At the surface they handed up the cage into the dinghy and were helped in.

Luke, alone in the boat, asked, "Well, what happened?"

"The rascal is too big for this cage. We are going to have to make a larger one."

"Rats!"

"Let's go back and get on it," said Laura.

"Right," replied Dan.

By the end of the day the cage had been enlarged hopefully enough to accommodate the huge moray.

That night, Dan kept the schedule with Nancy. She informed them that according to the number on the fuselage, the plane was one that had disappeared on its flight soon after the beginning of World War II. It was reported to be carrying unspecified cargo destined for Switzerland. The secret cargo was to be used to raise money for the Japanese war effort.

"Nancy, you have been of great service to us. We

insist that you come visit the island. We will make the arrangements for your visit. It will not cost you anything! How does that sound? Over."

"Oh, my," she gushed. "That would be utterly fantastic! I would be delighted to visit you and your island. Over."

"Great! It may take some time, but we will see to it. VS6XYL, this is NOAUZ. We will be clear with you now, and will continue to maintain the schedule as usual."

With that, they exchanged final reports and cleared with each other. Of course, as usual, a "pile-up" ensued. This time the rest of the family took turns working the horde of hams desiring to log a contact with the McKays. It was another fine evening for amateur radio.

At breakfast, on the east porch, they watched the tropical sunrise and conversed about Nancy's message and their plans for the day. They were in disagreement as to whether the pearls came from the wreck or not. The question was whether or not there was anything else remaining in the plane of value or interest. It was a good question, due to the fact that, although the Japanese were good divers, they did not have scuba gear and thus could not remain long in the plane on their dives just holding their breaths. It remained to be seen whether the Japanese had completely scoured the plane or not, and they all were anxious to find out.

Adam was on the dock near the O lab, filling the scuba tanks, when Susan stepped out.

"How's it going, Adam? You got that Moray yet?"

"No. We're taking a cage down that we had to enlarge this morning. Hope we get it this time."

"I'd like to see the site when you all get caught up and can work me in, okay?" asked Susan.

"Sure."

"Okay, then. See you later. Have a good day." She returned to the lab just as Dan arrived.

As Adam was loading their gear into the dingy, he spoke. "Dad, we need something more than this boat. Lots of people are interested in this wreck and want to see it. I just talked to Susan. She wants to go, and the chief said the Navy guys were all curious about the plane so...."

"You're right. I tell you what...tomorrow is Saturday. I'll talk to the chief about using one of the Navy's utility boats over the weekend. How's that? They use two of them to ferry people and goods between ship and shore. The smaller one would fit our purposes just fine."

"Sounds great, Dad."

"Okay then," said Dan, and turned toward the house and yelled, "Sarah, come on; it's your turn. We are ready to go."

"Coming."

Sarah was the last of the family to make the dive. She was anxious to see the plane.

Soon Adam, Dan and Sarah were over the wreck, preparing to take the cage down.

"Okay, now Sarah, when we get down there, you stand off a bit while I set the cage in place, then we will swim around the site and you can look in the windows.

Okay?"

"Right. I'm ready. Let's go!"

Dan grinned, "You are as anxious as the kids to get down there, I believe."

"You're right there."

So they slipped into the water, adjusted their masks and dove.

Sarah, the last of the family to learn to scuba dive, was still quite conscious of the water's pressure on her body and how she had to push against the pressure to breathe, but she had been handling the breathing well lately.

Upon their arrival at the site, Dan cautiously approached the open door and placed the cage as he had done before. Then they made the inspection of the site with Dan pointing out empty boxes strewn about the interior of the wreck.

He then touched Sarah's arm and when she turned toward him, he pointed upward.

As they ascended toward the surface keeping pace with their rising bubbles, Sarah could feel the pressure lessening on her body.

When they emerged and removed their masks, Sarah's only response was, "Interesting!"

Adam laughed. "Is that all you can say, Mom?"

"Well, we are not inside yet, are we?"

"Good point," agreed Adam.

"Let's get home and eat, then we will come back and check on the cage," said Dan.

"Sounds good to me," said Adam.

Minutes later they were back, tying up at the

dock.

"While you all are getting lunch ready, I am going to go talk to the chief."

"Okay, Dan. See you later. Thanks for taking me," said Sarah.

"My pleasure, my dear. See you all later."

A half hour later, Dan returned home.

"It's all set. We pick up the utility boat this evening and will have it all weekend," reported Dan.

"Outstanding!" said Luke. "Can I go with you to get it?"

"Guess so," replied Dan. "I will call you when the Navy's work day is over."

After lunch, Dan went back down to the Navy's camp and spent the afternoon with the Navy crew, surveying their progress. They were right on schedule. Dan was pleased with their professionalism, considering how young most of them were, and used every opportunity to tell them so. They had been on the job well over six months now and there had been no major injuries.

When it was time to stop work for the day, Dan called Luke on the handheld radio, "Come on down, Luke. We will ride out to the ship with the chief and pick up the utility boat."

"On my way."

While enroute to the ship, the chief said, "If you need anything on the dive site, let me know and if we have it, I will get it to you."

"Thanks, Chief. I may take you up on that."

An hour later, Dan and Luke arrived at the dock

with the utility boat, secured it to the dock, and headed up the path to the house.

"Good timing. Supper is ready," said Sarah.

"Yeah, my stomach told me that," Luke said, laughing.

"If the Moray will cooperate, we can have quite a crew on the dive site this weekend," said Dan. "Now let's pray and eat. I'm hungry, too."

That evening they tried to do some "hamming" but conditions were poor, so they soon gave it up failing to keep the sched with Nancy and invited the Ronamus and Jim Conrad and his staff to a marshmallow roast on the beach south of the dock. Because of the McKay family interest in oceanography, the evening was quite lively. Luke and Laura pressed the O team with questions until late in the evening.

"It has been a nice evening and tomorrow could be an eventful day, so we had better get some sleep," said Dan.

"Guess so," said Laura reluctantly. Oceanography was her passion.

"Goodnight. Thanks for inviting us to the roast. It was a nice evening," said Jim.

"Agreed," said the O crew.

The next morning, Saturday, began with a rain squall which threatened to curtail their planned dive on the wreck, but by midmorning the squall had passed the island by and in its wake was a beautiful tropical day!

After an early lunch, the O team, Ronamus and McKays gathered on the dock.

"If the Moray is not in the trap, then what will we do?" asked Laura.

"Guess we could cruise along the north side of the island for a bit. We don't know much about that area," suggested Dan. "Maybe pull into Oyster Bay."

"I just hope the Moray is in the trap," said Luke.

"We'll soon know. Let's get moving," said Dan.

Everyone but Luke clambered aboard, with Adam carrying Kamlani. Luke handed down all their gear and then hopped aboard.

Even with all the passengers and gear there was still plenty of room on the boat.

Dan pressed the starter button and the engine started, gently purring with a deep, powerful tone.

"I like the sound of this engine," said Luke.

"I agree with that, Luke," said Jim. "Music to my ears."

"Right. Now kick this baby, Dad, and let's get going!"

"Ever the impatient one," laughed Dan as he opened up to half throttle.

In a couple of minutes they were over the dive site.

"No use in our all going until we see if we have the eel. Come on, Adam. Let's go find out," ordered Dan.

"With you, Dad."

Over the side they went and slowly approached the wreck. As Adam waited a short distance away, Dan cautiously approached the cage.

Be in there, big guy.

When Dan was quite close to the cage, it began to shake violently.

Got it!

Dan turned and waved for Adam to join him, giving him a thumbs-up.

Adam joined his dad and slapped him on the back. Mission accomplished.

Carefully they eased the cage out of the plane and were amazed when they saw the size of the creature.

Slowly, slowly they ascended to the surface carefully avoiding placing fingers close to the caged fury.

When they got to the boat, even Susan was surprised at the size of the moray. "Why, it's larger than any of those in the sea cave."

"Let's get this guy back to the O tank and then we will head back here and check out the plane, finally," ordered Dan.

The awkwardness of towing the eel made slow going, but finally the job was done and they returned to the dive site.

Chapter Thirty
There's More?

"Well, let's pick a buddy and go check this out," said Dan.

Everyone geared up except the Ronamus, who had not yet been trained to scuba dive. However, Makko was quite capable of holding his breath and diving down for a few minutes if he had wanted to do so.

"Have fun. Maybe someday I will do scuba," murmured Kamlani.

"Of course you will," said a smiling Adam. With that the divers started their descent.

Jim Conrad remained in the boat with the Ronamus to keep the boat positioned above the divers.

The eight divers slowly descended to the wreck and immediately entered through the now unguarded hatch. They cautiously searched the interior of the plane to avoid stirring up the debris that had accumulated over time, but there was little to see until Luke signaled vigorously that he had found something under some particularly thick debris near the tail of the plane.

He pointed to some scratches on the floor around a small padlocked door. The Japanese had evidently tried to open the hatch, but had been unable to do so.

Dan examined the hatch, then pointed to Luke and hand signaled for him to go up and get something to pry open the small door.

He rose to the surface, pacing the bubbles from his regulator.

As he burst through the surface of the water, he shouted, "We found a locked door and need something to pry the lock off. Anything in the boat here that we could use to pry with?"

Makko and Sope scurried about the boat, rummaging through storage areas, and soon handed Luke a two-foot-long tapered iron bar.

"Thanks!" said Luke as he headed back down to the wreck.

When Dan saw what Luke had brought, he gave him a thumbs-up and a slap on the shoulder.

Because of the exposure to the ocean water, the hasp finally gave way and all gathered around as Dan tucked the iron bar underneath the door's edge and slowly raised it.

Dan grasped a lantern and carefully pointed it in the darkness. Seeing nothing, he pushed his head through the opening and slowly moved the beam of light around. It appeared to be empty except for what Dan thought to be a toolbox. He emerged from the hole and
handed the light to one of the onlookers. Then he tried to enter the hole, but he was too large. He straightened up and looked at the group gathered about him. It was obvious...Laura was the smallest, so if anyone could get through the hatch, she would be the one.

Dan pointed at Laura and then the hole. She understood and nodded that she would do it.

Because of the size of the hole, she would not be able to get through with her scuba gear on, but that was no problem. All the McKays knew how to hold their breath, remove their scuba equipment under water, and then put it back on again if necessary.

So Laura entered the hole feet-first, up to her waist. Dan lifted the air tank from her back. With the mouthpiece still in her mouth, she completely lowered herself into the dark space beneath the floor. Luke handed her a lantern and was able to get the tank down to her.

She flashed the light around and spotted the box sitting at an awkward angle about ten feet from the opening, jammed against the front bulkhead.

Fortunately, the box had a handle on each end, so it was easy for her to move it to the floor opening. She pushed one end of the box up toward the hole, where Luke swiftly pulled it up to the waiting group. Then he took Laura's tank from her and she followed it up through the hole with the mouthpiece again still in her mouth.

The divers were elated and patted Laura on the head. Then they all headed out of the plane and to the surface with their questionable prize.

As they were surfacing, the question on everyone's mind was what, if anything, was in this toolbox. Tools? They were soon to find out.

Chapter Thirty-one
The Tool Box

At the surface, Adam and Dan handed up the tool box to Makko, as Luke handed the pry bar up to Sope.

Makko dragged the box to the middle of the boat as the divers clambered aboard and gathered around.

"Hurry up, Dad! Pop the lid on this thing!" said Luke.

"Okay, Son. Take it easy. It's not going anywhere." Dan took his time as he stuck the pry bar under the padlock.

"Adam, stand on this while I give it a try."

Adam did as his father directed.

Dan paused for a moment, then gave the bar a quick, downward thrust. The hasp broke loose as Dan forced the lock up and the door was free. He looked around the circle of expectant faces and enjoyed the moment.

Grabbing the broken hasp, he lifted the door open to reveal the box's contents. There was little in the box except for a small wooden container about the size of a loaf of bread. It was so badly decomposed that it was soft to Dan's touch.

As he started to lift it out, it came apart in his hands, showering its contents all over the bottom of the tool box.

Suddenly there was pandemonium!

There, scattered in the bottom of the toolbox, were...**diamonds!**

"Well, we certainly have more to tell Nancy," commented Dan after all the group's adrenaline had been spent.

"Boy, do we ever!" agreed Luke.

Hardly anyone slept that night. Their minds were racing. Everyone present was to have a share of the results of the pearls and diamonds. What a page of the island's history this was!

Chapter Thirty-two
The Surgery

The second of December was the day that Kamlani, her mother and father, Dan and Adam would begin their journey to Honolulu for the hoped-for surgery.

In addition to the usual baggage, Adam also packed their backup portable HF transceiver. Hopefully it could be operated from or near the hospital. Tripler Army Hospital on Oahu, Hawaii was their destination.

The morning of December second was extraordinarily beautiful on McKay Island. Everything was just perfect on this special occasion.

Kamlani hugged everyone goodbye and was carried aboard the *Sarah* by Adam, who had just said his goodbyes to everyone remaining behind.

"I have a radio contact scheduled with KH6JPR in Hawaii at 8 am our time here. It will be 11 am there," said Dan. "Luke, monitor 14.260Mhz. That's where we were to make the contact. If we don't copy him, then maybe you can here."

"We'll be listening," said Luke. "He's supposed to let us know if everything is still a go for the operation on the tenth and whether you
can operate out of the hospital, right?"

"That's affirmative," said Dan. "Then switch to forty meters and call us on the boat to let us know what he has to say."

"Why switch to forty meters?" asked Kamlani,

who was just starting to learn about amateur radio.

"Well, because signals go up and strike a layer in the atmosphere that reflects it back down to the earth or water. The distance between the signals on forty meters would probably reach us better than on twenty meters, where it would probably go over us and we would not hear it," explained Adam.

"You draw me picture, okay?" asked Kamlani, smiling.

"Okay," laughed Adam.

There was plenty of help in casting off the mooring lines and shoving the Sarah away from the dock, and quite a number of tears.

The wind filled *Sarah's* sails and they were on their way.

As soon as they cleared the island, Dan turned to Kamlani, who was sitting in the cockpit by the wheel, and said, "Okay, young lady, I am going to put you to work. See the compass there? It's showing a bearing of 235 degrees. I want you to take the wheel and keep us pointed that way."

"Okay. I do it," said Kamlani with an enthusiastic smile.

The *Sarah* moved along smartly as they headed southwest, running before the prevailing northeast wind. While Dan secured everything on deck, Adam showed Sope how to cook for the crew in the galley below deck using the two-burner propane stove and the microwave.

The trip to Majuro, the capital of the Marshall Islands which had airline service to Honolulu, was pleasant and uneventful. Most of the time they had good, solid ham radio contacts with everyone back on the island. They learned that indeed the operation was scheduled, and that Adam could work the ham rig there.

When they arrived at the Majuro yacht basin, Dan maneuvered the boat to the dock expertly as usual, Adam noted.

A motorcyclist rapidly approached them.

"Hey, man! You want a ride to the airport?" he asked.

"No, not this time, but could you ride to the airport and have a taxi come get us?" asked Dan.

"Sure thing, Boss," and he was gone.

Soon they were in a taxi headed to the airport with Kamlani, awed by the fast-paced activity of the place.

As they approached the Pacific Airlines plane for Honolulu, Makko said, "Are you sure that big plane can get off the ground, Mr. McKay?"

"Yes, Makko, it can get us to Honolulu okay. Don't worry," said Dan.

The flight to Hawaii was smooth and the crew members were pleasant and professional.

As they approached Honolulu International, Dan could look out to the west and see the runway at Barber's Point Naval Air Station where he had been stationed in 1957-1958 flying WV-2 Super Constellations for AEWRON-14. He had been a part of the DEW (Distant Early Warning) line which stretched from Midway Island north to Alaska where the airborne radar overlapped the Alaskan ground radar. The naval air station was closed now, a victim of the many recent military base closings.

Dan thought how young he had been in those days before his tours in Vietnam, where he had been shot down twice, but not captured. He unconsciously placed his hand on his right thigh where the scar remained from one of the bullets that had taken him and his plane down.

They were met at the terminal by personnel from Tripler Army Hospital.

The staff made them feel welcome, and after an exhaustive examination, the doctors decided Kamlani was a good candidate for the surgery and that she would probably be able to walk again.

Early in the morning of the day for the surgery, Adam, Dan, Sope and Makko gathered at Kamlani's bedside, waiting for them to take her to surgery.

They circled her bed, held hands and bowed their heads as Dan prayed for the success of Kamlani's surgery.

When the moment arrived, Adam felt a tightening in his throat as they gave Kamlani a preliminary shot.

"It's going to be okay, Kamlani. We'll see you pretty soon, okay?" said Adam as he held on to her hand until they wheeled her away.

"Okay," she said, smiling confidently. A hug from her parents and she was gone.

The surgery took four hours. To Adam it seemed much longer, but he had been able to make contact with the island, which helped pass the time.

Eventually they were allowed into the recovery room, just as Kamlani was starting to become alert to her surroundings.

"The surgery went quite well," said the surgeon. "Now we will see if she has any response in her legs, though it may be too soon for that," he said, and began to run an instrument like a wand up and down the length of the bottom of her right foot, then the left. Nothing.

"We'll try again pretty soon. I thought it was probably too soon. I'll be back before long and try again."

"Hi," murmured Kamlani feeling the effects of the anesthesia. "I okay?"

"You fine," replied Sope. "You rest. We talk later."

"Yes, Mother."

Then she turned to Adam and smiled.

Adam grinned broadly. "Welcome back, Kamlani," he said softly.

"My legs okay?" she asked.

"We will know as soon as the doctor comes back in a few minutes," Adam replied.

Soon the doctor returned and said, "Hello, young lady. You're looking good. Now let's see if your feet and legs want to move."

Again he repeated the procedure, and barely, but noticeably, one of her toes moved!

"Yes," breathed Adam and squeezed her hand.

As the minutes passed, more and more of the

toes, then the feet, and finally the legs moved.

Adam bowed his head for a moment and silently thanked God for the successful surgery.

Kamlani mended remarkably quickly. A week after the surgery, she was on her feet holding onto the rails in physical therapy.

Adam had been "hamming" the whole time, giving everyone back on the island frequent accounts of Kamlani's progress. Hams all over the world had been listening and contacting Adam with their support. Kamlani was becoming an international figure!

Two weeks to the day after her surgery, Kamlani could walk, slowly, unassisted.

It was time to go home.

The flight from Honolulu to Majuro was cloudless and smooth. Kamlani would rest awhile, look out the window awhile, then rest again repeatedly until they landed.

The boat trip to McKay Island was also smooth, and just before the island started to emerge from the sea, a dot appeared in the sky and quickly grew larger. It was the Cub. It dropped down close to the boat, making a pass by at about thirty feet off the water.

"Look!" said Adam. "It's Mom and Laura!" All on board the boat waved vigorously as the plane made several more passes, then headed back toward the island.

It was late afternoon when the yacht approached the dock, again one of those precious moments in the tropics when everything was just simply perfect!

All those gathered on the dock gave a mighty cheer when Kamlani slowly stood up in the bow and waved.

Adam assisted her from the boat to the dock, where she was swallowed in a sea of well-wishers.

"We are having a welcome-back luau tonight," said Sarah. "You rest for a while, then we will start the luau, okay?"

"Okay," murmured Kamlani shyly.

While the travelers rested, the others made the final preparations for the party. It was to be on the beach just south of the dock, where the beach turns west. It was perfect; the beach, the palm trees, the water, the food, and the friends who loved Kamlani!

There was even going to be music, courtesy of the Navy that had gathered a group together to play for the occasion. Their talent, it turned out, was surprisingly good.

Slowly, people began to arrive: the Navy personnel, the O team, the McKays, and finally Kamlani with her family and Adam.

It was a glorious evening with a lot of good-natured clowning, laughter and story-telling. The music was just superb.

The last event of the evening was the final song, "Sweet Leilani," sung by all who knew it.

And...Kamlani slowly rose to her feet, smiling, and very gently danced the hula to the music. There was not a dry eye on the entire island!

Chapter Thirty-three
The Pearl and Diamond Dealers

The next day after the luau, along toward evening, Dan was on the ham radio calling for Nancy in Hong Kong. "CQ, CQ, CQ, this is N0AUZ calling VS6XYL on schedule. Do you copy, Nancy?"

Immediately: "N0AUZ, this is VS6XYL. Solid copy, Dan. You are a solid 5-9 here in Hong Kong. What's going on there? Over."

"VS6XYL, this is N0AUZ returning. Fine business, Nancy. You are 5-9 here also. Well, the news here is that the surgery for the girl I was telling you about went extremely well. In fact, she danced the hula at her welcome-home party last night. So, how is it going with you? Over."

"This is VS6XYL. Oh, I guess my news is that I have made several telephone contacts here with the people you might be interested in. They are interested, but you would have to come here to meet with them. Over."

"VS6XYL, this is N0AUZ...I copy. I probably will come there, but we will have to talk it over here first. Would you be able to be on frequency tomorrow at this time? By the way, I really appreciate your help. So, back to you, Nancy. N0AUZ."

"This is VS6XYL. Roger on the schedule for tomorrow, Dan. Give everyone my best 73s. This is my final. You can wrap it up. N0AUZ, this is VS6XYL. I am clear and QRT.

"Roger. Have a pleasant day and 73s. VS6XYL, this is N0AUZ. I'm clear and QRT also."

The rest of the family had been listening to the ham radio conversation and urged Dan to go as soon as possible.

"Well, okay then, but let's see...how do I get there?" Dan thought for a moment then said, "How does this sound? I fly the Cub to Majuro, take a commercial flight to Guam, then fly from there to Hong Kong."

"Sounds all right to me," said Sarah. "Guys?"

Yes, that would work, they agreed.

The next night Dan kept the schedule with Nancy. He said he had her address from the amateur radio call book and would look her up, but that he had no idea when that would be as he could not schedule airline flights from the island. Also, he asked her to notify the buyers that he was coming. It was no problem for her because she had an answering machine. So it was done. He was on his way.

Chapter Thirty-four
Hong Kong

Next morning the McKays rose early. While Sarah and Laura prepared breakfast, Dan and the boys carefully examined the Cub.

The flight to Majuro was going to require good piloting by Dan, as Majuro was close to the maximum range that the Cub could fly. Careless flying could mean running out of gas before getting there.

One thing in Dan's favor was that he would have a tailwind, which would allow him to stretch out the miles per gallon if it held. Coming back would be a different story….

When it was time to go, they all stood on the dock and had a group hug, or "family hug" as they called it.

"See you all in a few days," said Dan as he climbed into the rear seat and buckled in.

"We'll be here," replied Sarah as she had said so many times in their naval career.

Adam spun the prop, and the Cub purred to life. Wasting no time, Dan quickly went through the pre-takeoff check, then turned into the wind, waved one last time, and pushed the throttle full forward. The Cub soon was at takeoff speed and smoothly cleared the water. Airborne!

The sun had not yet touched the island, so at one thousand feet Dan met the rising sun and gazed down at the dark sea from his sunlight position. It was the time of day he enjoyed the most and this was a pleasurable experience for sure.

The flight was pleasant and uneventful. Radio contact with the handheld had lasted until he was out of range about an hour into the flight.

Three and a half hours later Dan approached the coast of Majuro. At a height of one thousand feet, he could see the commercial airport where he needed to go after he landed.

Fortunately, it was not far from the water and there was ample room for him to land inside the breakwater where the marina was located.
Making a pass to make sure there was nothing in the way, he brought the little plane in for a landing. The float needle in the gas tank showed that he still had some gas remaining, but not much.

He taxied up to the marina, tied up to the dock, and made inquiries as to where he could safely leave the Cub for a few days. The manager assured him that he had a safe, secure place for it. He was pleased to have the plane in his marina.

The same cyclist they had seen on their way to Kamlani's operation asked Dan if he wanted a ride. Dan took him up on it, and was soon speeding down the road riding behind the local on his motorcycle, trying desperately to hang on to his suitcase and his carry-on bag containing some of the pearls and diamonds. Most had been left behind as there were just too many to bring them all. Of course, he had the large black one and the large white one and some of the various cuts of diamonds.

They arrived at the airport with Dan still tightly clutching his luggage to his chest.

His body felt like one huge cramp as he approached the ticket counter.

"May I help you?" asked the man behind the counter, trying not to laugh at a man in obvious physical discomfort.

"I hope so. I need a flight to Guam as soon as possible."

"You are in luck. That flight doesn't go very often, but today is the day."

"How much time do I have before it goes?"

"About two hours. You hungry? We have a place to eat here or you can probably get a ride to some of the eating places on down the road." Then, smiling, the attendant said, "The guy you rode here with would be glad to take you."

"I'll eat here."

Dan sat around the lobby, dozing and reading two-year-old magazines until time for the flight.

The plane was a 727-200 commercial jet, which seemed huge to Dan after being in the Cub all morning. The flight crew was a quite informal group. Before they left the ground, the pilot already knew Dan had been a Navy pilot in Vietnam just as he had been.

Dan told them quite a bit about his island so when they took off, they flew a little to the east of their normal flight route and flew over the island.

"Nice-looking island," said the pilot to Dan, who was sitting in the co-pilot's seat on the right side of the cockpit. "I may have to drop in on you someday."

"We would love that," said Dan. "Really. I am going to expect to see you down there one of these days." Looking down as the pilot dipped the right wing, he could see everything except who was who.

"Very well, Captain. You have a deal."

"Say," said Dan. "I have my hand-held ham radio in my carry-on bag. Would it be possible for me to give them a call down there?"

"No problem, Dan. I am a ham, too—something else we have in common. Go for it."

Quickly Dan pulled the radio out of the bag.

"KB0FKI, this is N0AUZ. Copy?"

After the third repeat, Sarah answered, "N0AUZ, this is KB0FKI. Dan, what a surprise. I did not expect to hear from you like this. What do you know? Over."

"Hi, Sarah. I'm flying over the top of you now. Look up! The Cub and I made it okay. This flight crew is treating me like a king. I invited them to the island soon."

They chatted for a while, then... "Dan. We...(static)...you...Thursday..."

The jet had taken them far enough apart that the conversation was abruptly ended.

"Wonder what that was all about?" mused Dan. "Thursday? Oh, well."

The flight took about nine hours, with four stops along the way, and it was dark when they landed at Guam International Airport. By the end of the flight, Dan was well acquainted with all five of the crew.

Well, thought Dan, shaking hands with them as he left the plane, *I think the guest list is growing, and*

I'm just getting started. Guess I'll just have to quit being so friendly. Ha.

Dan's luck held and he was soon airborne again, but this flight crew was not so informal; courteous, but not informal.

The flight arrived in Hong Kong at midday and after the slow, calm pace of his island, Dan felt somewhat stressed to be confronted with the teeming mass of humanity that swarmed through the Hong Kong flight terminal.

"Mr. McKay. Paging Mr. McKay. Call operator 14 on one of the courtesy phones, please."

Dan was startled to hear his name over the PA system. The courtesy phones were abundant and he lifted the nearest one.

"Operator 14, please."

The operator directed him to a specified location where he was met by Nancy and a representative of the pearl buyers who chauffeured him to a hotel that they had chosen for him. There the meetings would take place.

"Nancy, you have no idea what a great help you have been for all of us on the island," said Dan as they drove through the crowded streets. "And how did you know I was going to be here today?"

"Easy. I kept the usual contact schedule and Adam told me you were on your way. And it's no big deal, Dan, as far as my help is concerned," she replied.

"By the way, what do you do here in Hong Kong?"

"I teach school for the children of the American

businessmen and women who live here."

"Great! Well, as we have said before, we expect you to come visit us soon...perhaps when your school is out for the summer," suggested Dan. "Who knows...we may have a teaching job for you on the island someday."

"That sounds wonderful," replied Nancy. "That sure would be a switch from here."

The meeting was held later that evening after Dan had a chance to refresh. After the introductions, they all sat around an oval table where Dan proceeded to pass around the pearl and diamond samples.

"There are more, gentlemen. Many, many more. Their quality is consistent with these I brought here." He then told them specifically how many there were when one of them asked for the figure.

Nancy was amazed by the quality and amount of the island's treasure displayed before her.

After a lengthy, careful consideration and inspection, Dan and Nancy were asked to leave them for a time so they could consult with their various firms and consider whether they had the means and desire to compete for the purchase of the prize Dan was offering for sale.

After a short time, Dan and Nancy were ushered back into the room.

Each group handed Dan a sealed envelope that contained their potential offering.

"Thank you, gentlemen. I shall take these to my room and study them carefully. Then, I will contact you....probably later this evening. Thanks again," said

Dan.

With Nancy, he hurried to his room, eager to examine the contents of the sealed envelopes. After reading the notes from each firm, Dan decided on the offer of a Mr. Woo, who also offered to invest in any tourist ventures on the island if the McKays should happen to have an interest in that direction.

One more day in Hong Kong was needed. Nancy showed him some of the city while Mr. Woo spent the day conferring with his organization. It was their feeling that he should go to McKay Island and make an offer on the island's treasures after viewing it all first hand. Mr. Woo would fly to McKay Island two weeks later.

The following day, Dan was on his way home, which seemed more and more like home to him every day. Nancy had assured him she would visit them when it was possible for her to do so.

Dan stepped off the 727 in Majuro and was immediately offered a ride to the marina, this time in a Jeep. It was 2 p.m. when Dan got to the Cub. Thanks to the aid of the man in the Jeep, he was able to purchase aviation gas at the airport. He filled the Cub's gas tank as full as he could then strapped a five gallon can of gasoline into the empty front seat which under normal circumstances would be a bad idea.   He tied a rope around the float next to the dock so that when he pulled the propeller to start the engine, the rope would hold the plane in against the dock until he could get in and release the rope. It went well, and soon the Cub was humming its song as Dan taxied out, checked the engine ignition, then gave it full throttle for takeoff.

He did not fly a pattern, but cleared the water already on a heading for the island. He flew at only thirty feet off the water to create a lifting effect on the Cub and extend the range of the plane.

Dan was stationed at NAS Barber's Point when a twin-engine Navy prop plane bound from Los Angeles to Honolulu had an engine explode from a runaway prop and could not hold altitude. When the plane settled almost to the water, it quit sinking and held its altitude just a few feet off the water. It also flew farther than it was thought to be able to do. It made it to Hilo, Hawaii on one good engine and fumes remaining. They later termed the phenomena the "T effect."

There was some wind, but it was light, which pleased Dan. *This will help the gas situation also. One thing is for sure, we must get a plane with more range than this old girl.*

Occasionally he called on the handheld radio. Because of his low altitude, he was near the island before he was able to make contact.

"KBOFKI. This is NOAUZ. Do you copy?"

Immediately there was a response.

"NOAUZ, this is KBOFKI. Read you pretty good. Where are you, Dad?" asked Adam.

"I would say almost home. I'm flying at thirty feet. Keep an eye out for me because I will be cutting it pretty close on fuel."

"We will be watching and standing by."

"Okay. Well, I am not going to chat as I want to save my batteries, so I am clear and standing by. KBOFKI, NOAUZ."

Soon after their conversation, the wind stopped completely, and Dan brought the Cub home as twilight began to settle on the island.

He sat the Cub down in the quiet water of the lagoon, with less than a gallon of fuel remaining.

Soon after his arrival home, the usual group met in the McKay's great room, where Dan shared his trip experiences with them.

"...and Mr. Woo also expressed an interest in investing in any money-making ventures we might pursue, such as a tourist hotel, or diving, or a plantation. That sort of thing. I made no commitments along those lines. I told him that would be up to both future owners of the island. Of course, the O team has a say about the diamond sale, as you get a share of that part of the sale."

Sarah was the first to voice her opinion. "No! I for one do not want this place to become a commercial, money-grabbing island. I say no. And when he gets here I will tell him so."

No one disagreed, but rather vocally seconded her strong response.

"I told him that would be your reaction," Dan said, laughing heartily. "Now the question is, can we live here and own this island and remain unexploited? There are many things that we will be considering soon. How will we provide for our food? Do we become a country? Will we have a flag? Dual citizenship? A constitution? A new country for amateur radio operators to add to their list? What else will the island reveal to us in time? And on and on. Got you thinking, huh?"

"Dad," said Adam.

"Yes, Adam."

"You definitely have me thinking," replied Adam.

Kamlani shyly looked down at her hands and smiled.

To be continued...

Made in the USA
Columbia, SC
24 July 2022